MURDER IN MARYLAND

Books by Leslie Ford

THE SOUND OF FOOTSTEPS
BY THE WATCHMAN'S CLOCK
MURDER IN MARYLAND

Leslie Ford

MURDER

IN

MARYLAND

WILDSIDE PRESS

Murder in Maryland

Published by Wildside Press LLC
www.wildsidepress.com

TO
BRYANT BUSH KINGSBURY

MURDER IN MARYLAND

CHAPTER

I

JUDGE GARTH'S cold, ancient gray eyes met mine searchingly across the dusty ink-stained green baize top of his office table. A solitary blue-bottle barged in crazy circles, buzzing angrily, against the dingy window.

"Human life, Dr. Fisher," he said in his relentless monotonous voice, "is sacred. Even women doctors must know that."

"And I do know it, Judge Garth," I answered, meeting his grim appraising scrutiny calmly. "If I'd got to Miss Wyndham's in time to save her, I'd have done it—no matter what my personal feelings were. But I'm concerned chiefly with life, Judge Garth. I'm more moved when I hear the first cry of a new-born baby than I am at the rattle of death in an old man's throat. That's why I'm not sorry Miss Wyndham's dead. Other people can live now."

Not a muscle moved in the lean fine old face across from me.

"She was dead, then, when you got there?"

"She was; had been, probably, for several hours.

Daphne Lake, a hairdresser at Bess Chew's beauty shop, telephoned for me. Miss Wyndham was dead."

"Miss Wyndham was murdered."

A flicker in the stony eyes, levelled, probing, not three feet from mine, was all that betrayed that Judge Garth had any memory of young Tom Garth wandering hand in hand with Nettie Wyndham, lost in the young sweetness of the magnolia-filled dusk of a long-ago Spring.

"I guessed she was," I said, "when I saw the upset glass on the table and the dog lying there."

I couldn't help a shudder at the thought of that horrible hairless little beast, obese and rheumy-eyed. It had hardly left the old woman's side for eighteen years.

"Do you know who murdered Antoinette Wyndham, Dr. Fisher?"

Judge Garth's thin set lips scarcely moved to ask the question.

I shook my head.

"I don't. I don't know who did it."

I didn't . . . not then.

My conversation with Judge Garth was several days after the day they unveiled the bronze tablet on the doorstep of the Wyndham house in Charles Street. In the light of what happened later, the unveiling of that tablet became as perfectly planned a first act as in a Belasco production. Everything that made the drama of the Wyndhams—tragedy or melodrama, depending on Judge Garth's view or mine—was there when the curtain went up.

There was the house; a beautiful old red brick Georgian mansion with elaborately carved door and Palladian window, a perfect symbol of the past glories of the Wyndhams, and of their possessions, past and present. Wyndham House, hidden away behind a high brick wall and a high box maze, is a living mystery to the town. That day—it was early in October—when old Miss Nettie, who lived there alone with her horrible little dog and one old Negro servant, opened the gates, people came in who had not been there since the last time they were opened, seventeen years before. That time was for Gail Wyndham's father, when he went out on his last journey to St. Margaret's Churchyard. The next day Gail and her mother went on foot by the wicket at the bottom of the garden. Gail was then three.

Since then the big gates had been barred and bolted. A few people entered by the wicket. Miss Nettie and the Mexican hairless bitch hobbled out sometimes after dusk, and went as far as the post-box on the corner. They never spoke. The day the bronze tablet was unveiled was the first time most of the people present had heard Miss Nettie speak, or had seen her in the daylight, for seventeen years.

She stood on the small porch, framed by the lovely elaborately carved white doorway like a grotesque figure from a fairy book—wizened and brown as a russet apple that's been in the cellar a dozen years, sharp and beady-eyed as some small hungry rodent. She was dressed in an ancient heavy black silk, brocaded with purple morning-glories. The amethyst collar round her withered throat caught the sun in a thousand shafts of glorious, deep purple light. An old-fashioned diamond pin sparkled on the tight-fitting black bodice. She supported her thin wiry body by a heavy thorn stick grasped tightly in one bony hand. The other clutched the bent arm of her handsome nephew, Richard Wyndham.

At Miss Nettie's right, a few feet from her, stood Gail Wyndham, Richard's cousin; age twenty, tall and slim, with a head like some dark, tropical flower. She was holding the corsage of orchids that the State Regent had presented her aunt; and I was just thinking how few women can really manage orchids, and how perfectly they suited Gail's rather exotic beauty, when the old woman turned and deliberately snatched them from the girl's hand, rapping her leg with the stick as she did so.

A little gasp in the audience clustered about the steps on the lawn brought a flush to Gail's pale ivory cheeks, Miss Nettie darted a savage, angry glance about her. Richard Wyndham, at her side, merely raised one eyebrow ever so slightly, and the mocking smile in his dark, handsome face deepened a moment.

Two other members of the family saw it. Eliot Wyndham, in the fringe of the crowd near me, flushed darkly and bit his lip. His older brother, Chase, standing near Judge Garth on the other side of the path, brushed a speck off the lapel of his immaculate double-breasted jacket.

Some people in town, Alice Penniman particularly, had thought that Miss Nettie was taking the occasion of this unveiling to make a more or less public gesture of restitution to the children of her two dead brothers.

"There'd be no other point in bringing Chase and Eliot down from New York, or asking Gail to stand with her on the porch," Mrs. Penniman, briskly practical, had said. "If she intended to leave everything she's got, even the jewels—which personally I don't believe exist—, to that precious Richard Wyndham, then she'd have him there and none of the others."

After the incident of the orchids I caught her eye across the crowd. Miss Nettie was pretty obviously taking the occasion to show her niece and two nephews, and everyone else present, that she hadn't changed in the least. She clung to Richard Wyndham's arm, looked proudly up into his dark face. And he, I must say, played his rôle of dutiful, loving nephew flawlessly.

I've never liked Richard Wyndham, but I must admit there's something quite breath-taking about his mocking brown eyes and clean-cut forehead and high imperious nose. Most women find him irresistible—some to their misfortune. He was charming that morning, as he patted his aunt's scrawny, be-ringed fingers, and bent down, affectionately protec-tive, to catch her waspish comments from time to time.

When the State Regent spoke of Miss Nettie's splendid example in cherishing and preserving the past glories of the town, he squeezed her hand and smiled down at her. Tears of happiness blurred the old woman's eyes, and I found myself thinking that after all . . . At least I did until I caught a glimpse of the impassive marble countenance of Judge Garth. Then I felt suddenly that I'd been moved by something tawdry and false.

Everyone there knew that Miss Nettie adored her nephew, and that she'd willed him the entire Wynd-ham estate: house, furniture, tobacco lands, stocks and bonds, the family jewels. She had long ago made a will to that effect. Once each year she sum-moned her latest lawyer and had him read it aloud. The reading had once taken place in front of Gail and her three cousins.

"I just want them to know," cackled Miss Nettie to a friend who spread it through town, "that they'll get nothing from me. It's my Ricky that's been a stay and a prop to me. He knows what an old woman likes."

Everybody had hoped that something would change Miss Nettie's mind. The incident of the orchids was evidence enough that nothing had. Although there was something odd about that.

I've always known how conflicting the testimony of bystanders is, but never to the extent that it turned out to be in the Wyndham case. When it was found that old Miss Nettie had not just died, but had been murdered, it was also found that the jewels reputed to be in the family had disappeared. Mr. Taylor, the State's Attorney, called in various people who had been present at the unveiling, many of whom had shaken old Miss Nettie's hand before they left. No two of them had taken away the same mental picture of the scene on the porch.

Old Mrs. Turner, for instance, swore on oath that Gail had snatched the orchids from her aunt. Mrs. Jacok said the girl had on an expensive pale yellow silk suit. She actually was wearing a white wool Golflex dress of mine, which she'd skillfully cut down from a 42 to a 36 for the occasion. Miss Arnold said Miss Nettie was dressed in black alpaca and wore no jewels. Mrs. Turner said the dead woman had on rubies as well as amethysts; and told me privately the other day that, come to think of it, she also remembered seeing the pearls. Whether on Gail or her aunt she couldn't remember. I suggested that perhaps Richard had worn them, but she said she thought not. It was either Miss Nettie or Gail.

Some people remembered Miss Nettie as looking paler than usual, others as more robust. Few of them, as a matter of fact, had so much as seen her for years. Old Mr. Nelson Jacok plainly saw Gail cast her aunt the most malevolent look he'd ever seen on 'human woman. To be sure Miss Nettie had her faults but she was a lady to her fingertips. The majority of people agreed that Miss Nettie had on some purple ornaments and a green ring. Her old friends, and some who had only heard of the family treasure, insisted that she had worn jewels worth a king's ransom. Mrs. Bassett said that to people who never saw jewels, the truck she'd worn no doubt appeared very grand.

At any event, the State regarded their testimony as sufficient evidence that at least a few of the missing jewels were still about, and conducted an investigation accordingly. But that was later.

While the State Regent was still speaking, I was thinking what a shame it was to leave that house, and the almost priceless furniture in it, to the handsome scoundrel on the porch, when Gail had nothing except $50 a month that Alice Penniman paid her as a sort of social secretary, when someone touched my elbow from behind. I didn't need to turn to hear Nat Penniman's perfectly audible whisper: "That guy gives you a pain in the neck. Look at him!"

The girl standing bare-headed in front of me stiffened perceptibly, and a faint rosy flush spread over the white skin between the collar of her starched linen uniform and the gleaming coil of blonde hair on her neck. She didn't turn around, however. She was intent on the unveiling business now in full swing on the porch.

When Miss Nettie drew aside the flag that covered the tablet, and the State Regent read the account on it of the fame of the first Wyndham, Richard glanced over our way. There was an exciting flicker in his mocking dark eyes that obviously wasn't meant for me or any of the other middle-aged women around me. Several people, women mostly, turning disapproving eyes on the little hairdresser, suddenly caught my eye over her blonde head, and nodded as graciously as possible on such short notice. If Richard Wyndham had a special interest in Daphne Lake, it's of course his business —and hers. In fact I should say she was the one person in town able to cope with such a situation and come out ahead of the game. She always struck me as being an intelligent young person, in spite of that astonishing platinum blonde hair and perfectly shameless make-up that she doesn't need and never will.

When Richard Wyndham accepted the tablet on behalf of his aunt, and—ironically enough—his cousins, Daphne Lake glanced at her wrist-watch. Then she drew her beige lapin coat closer about her slight body and looked around. I nodded, and Nat Penniman said, "Hullo, Miss Lake!"

The girl smiled at me, and let her clear brown eyes that contrast so sharply with her amazing hair look right through and completely beyond Nat Penniman.

"May I get past, Dr. Fisher, please?" she whispered. "I've got an eleven o'clock appointment at the shop."

I moved aside. She made her way through the few straggling spectators behind us, and went quickly down the brick path. Nat Penniman, rather red, and Richard Wyndham weren't the only ones who watched her go.

Eliot Wyndham, edging closer to me, moved into the space she had left.

"Who is that girl, Dr. Fisher?" he asked after we had shaken hands.

"Her name's Daphne Lake," I said. "She works in a beauty shop down the road."

"A local girl?"

I shook my head.

"No. She's been here about six months. Why?"

Somehow one doesn't expect Eliot Wyndham to be interested in platinum blondes. He teaches at a woman's college in the North. His brother Chase, a New York broker, has a well-known roving eye. In fact, he's rather like his cousin Richard, except that he was not considered likely to get the family swag.

"No reason," Eliot said with a smile. "Except that she's very pretty."

He hesitated. The smile faded abruptly, as if it had been wiped off with a wet cloth.

"Is that the girl they say Richard's gone on?"

I recognized the idiom.

"He could do a lot worse," I said shortly. I liked Daphne Lake, and I didn't like Richard Wyndham.

"And she a lot better," he returned, "from all accounts."

The ceremony was over. Nat Penniman, still standing by me, said, "Look, lady doctor"—which he always calls me, to my great annoyance—"Mother's over there. She wants to speak to you."

"How is she?" I asked. "She looks better than she did yesterday."

Nat shrugged with the tolerance of twenty-four for the ills of middle-age.

"If she doesn't bust herself this noon. . . . She's finally crashed the Wyndhams. They're coming up to lunch. You'd think we were entertaining the Great Khan. Dad told me to ask you to get her to cut it out. She'll be having another attack."

I glanced across at the robust, vigorous figure of Alice Penniman, talking to Judge Garth, and holding a sort of general court for people coming down from shaking hands with Miss Nettie and the State Regent. No one knew better than I what having the Wyndhams to lunch meant to Alice, unless it was her son, standing there with his pipe in his mouth, his lean, strong, young frame hung with a curious outfit made out of grayish tan tweed. He was obviously worried about her.

"When did all this happen?"

"She's been at Gail ever since that old scarecrow decided to let them stick the plaque on her house. You know how much influence Gail has there. Well,

Mother's as determined as any Wyndham ever was. When she once makes up her mind, it's made."

He frowned and shifted his empty pipe to his pocket.

"Mother kept at it, and last night the poor kid gave in. Said she'd ask that guy up there to get the old lady to come. She would if he asked her, and Mother knew it. So Gail had to call him up and ask him. Didn't she tell you about it?"

"I haven't seen her."

Gail lives with me, and sends out my bills and writes my letters for her room, breakfast, and dinner. It's the Wyndham pride that wouldn't let her live at the Pennimans'. That or her aunt.

"So they're coming, the whole lot of 'em—*and* Cousin Richard. You know, I'm damned if I see how Mother stomachs that crowd. We've been here eighteen years, and she's tried all the time to make the old woman. She's been in this house once. *Once*, mind you. Yet that old raven's as important to her as . . ."

Not being able to think of anything, he let it go. "Look, she's beckoning to us. Can you come over?"

We went over. Mrs. Penniman was talking to Chase Wyndham.

"Hello, Chase—it's nice to see you back. How's New York?"

"Much the same, Doctor. Something's got to happen, and nothing seems to."

"Isn't it terrible?" said Mrs. Penniman. "Ruth, have you heard that Miss Wyndham is coming to lunch? You and Judge Garth are coming too. Yes, you are. I tried to phone you last night. I won't take no. You're coming."

"Alice," I said, "I'd love to come. But I've just got too many people that need pills."

Going to lunch at Eliot House with that old raven, as Nat called her, was the last thing I wanted ever to do. I'd rather attend a plague.

"You *must* come. I've counted on you."

I shook my head. I can be as determined, when the occasion demands, as Mrs. Penniman or Miss Nettie either.

"Then I'll have an attack," she said briskly. She's the most exasperating woman in the world, and I'm devoted to her. "You'll have to come then."

"You won't have another one," I said. That was, as I knew very well, probably a lie. Her pseudo-angina condition made her subject to them whenever she got worked up over anything.

And I shouldn't have gone, if at that moment a light touch on my arm and a pair of dark pleading eyes looking up at me hadn't made me change my mind.

"Please come, Dr. Fisher," Gail Wyndham said very softly. "Please . . . I'll need you."

I looked at the girl. She was really frightened, under the waxen pallor of her face.

"All right, Alice," I said, turning back to Mrs.

Penniman, who was talking to some other people who'd come up. "I'll come to luncheon."

She looked at me in surprise.

"Of course you will, dear. Did somebody say you weren't?"

CHAPTER

2

THE position of a woman doctor in any small town is anomalous enough, but in a small southern town where there's still a definite notion that there are some things a lady doesn't do, her position is still more curious. For years I treated whooping cough, measles, and mumps in the very young. Later I was called in for impoverished adults who couldn't afford anything better. I had a scattering of the "better" people for colds and indiscretion in eating. Eventually, by the death of two of our older doctors, I succeeded to the practice of respectable diseases (if any disease is respectable). That's the amusing part of small towns and their doctors. A man, no matter how bad, is better than a woman. A woman doctor who's been with you twenty years, however, is better than a young male doctor who's just come to town, no matter how good he is.

So in the twenty years since I first hung out my shingle and bound up my first fractured arm, I've got to know the people of this town very well indeed. There's really not much about the lives of his

—or her—patients that a doctor in a small town doesn't know. It's an acid test of both of them.

Alice Penniman was a patient of mine, one of my earliest and certainly my wealthiest. She had what we call a pseudoangina pectoris. As she expresses it, "It's a perfectly beastly bad heart there's nothing wrong with at all"—which of course isn't exactly true. It's a nervous condition, although looking at Mrs. Penniman, robust, blonde and vigorous, it seems absurd to think of her as neurotic. It's a broad term, as doctors use it, and if you know Alice you realize that there's something in her that drives an apparently intelligent woman to almost insane lengths, at times, to get what she wants; or to keep somebody else from getting it, if the cat happens to jump that way. And no one can ever say which way it's going to be—least of all her family. Her family, consisting of one husband and one son, publicly and at all times bear witness to the fact that Mother is extravagant, flighty, has a finger in every pie baked in the entire state, gets hipped on every fad that comes along, in fact is little short of a cross borne with good-natured tolerance. Actually, they think there's nobody like Mother. Whatever she does is, as their colored cook puts it, "white with a blue rim around it."

I thought very differently about it when I shut up shop, a few minutes before one, and got into my car to go up to Eliot House for lunch.

What Nat Penniman had said about his mother

was perfectly true—truer than he knew. He wasn't
in a position to see how the Wyndham idea had
grown until it had become a mild mania with her.
It started when Alice Penniman decided she wanted
a colonial house and colonial furniture, and further
decided that it was the Wyndham house and the
Wyndham furniture that she wanted. Mr. Penniman, who made millions in asbestos, set out to buy
them. Miss Nettie not only refused to sell. She
ordered the Pennimans out of the house, brandish-
ing her thorn stick at them.

Alice Penniman, who could afford to bide her
time—after all, Miss Nettie was sixty then, and as
frail-looking as Alice was robust—bought the Eliot
house on the Hill, did it over, collected old furniture, and waited for Miss Nettie to die. I don't
think Alice has ever bought a chair, a chest, or a
piece of crown derby that she hasn't said, "I simply
had to have it, it will go divinely in the Wyndham
drawing room." Thus she practically lived in
Wyndham House, though actually she'd been in it
just once, and that twenty years ago, when Miss
Nettie ran her and her astonished husband out. But
Alice Penniman was not the woman to say die, and
Miss Nettie apparently was not the woman to do it.

Alice's getting Miss Nettie out of her house in the
middle of the day to lunch in her own house was at
once more of a feat and less of a feat than her son
thought. Miss Nettie, with that idolatrous devotion
to her precious nephew, would do anything he asked

her—except, perhaps, receive the Pennimans in Wyndham House. She might even have done that. And Alice, I know, had thought before of intriguing through him. Pride had prevented that. After all, the wealthiest woman in town could hardly stoop to asking such favors of a young man without visible means of support and with a reputation of town loafer and gambler on horses, cards and women. I wouldn't be surprised, in fact, if Alice Penniman didn't recognize something potentially dangerous, even for a woman of her age, in his dark mocking eyes and firm sensuous mouth. Alice really needed an asbestos husband to take care of her periodically.

It wasn't so much that she couldn't have worked on Richard to get her away with old Nettie. It was Gail that she couldn't manage.

Gail had become her social secretary first because Alice felt genuinely sorry for her and knew she needed some such job; and second, because, in that way doing something for a Wyndham, she felt that Miss Nettie must eventually soften. Alice was shamelessly frank about it. Gail had been with her since she finished high school at sixteen. She had lived with me since she entered high school. She had the fierce pride of the Wyndhams, and was as stubborn and inflammable as her aunt, whom she hated as much as her aunt apparently hated her. I've seen the child turn white with rage at hardly more than the mere mention of her aunt's name. She also had an intense dislike, which sometimes seemed to me

akin to fear, of her cousin Richard. How Alice ever
got her to speak to him, to ask him to have their
aunt come to the Pennimans' for lunch, I didn't
know till later. Alice isn't always exactly scrupu-
lous.

Half-way up the hill, just in back of the town,
I met Judge Garth. He was walking up to the Pennimans' very slowly, his head bent, stopping now
and then to rest. I drew up beside him.

"May I give you a lift," I said.

He looked up, surprised. There aren't many people in town who'd dare speak to him unless he spoke
first.

"Why, thank you," he said, with a reasonably
affable smile. "That's kind of you. This hill is getting too much for me. I used to walk it easily. Age
has its penalties."

"Most people think it has nothing else," I replied.

"Because they haven't learned to slow down, and
meet death half-way."

I glanced aside at the stern old jurist. I was very
much amazed at the gentle, almost benign quality
of his side face. The thin iron lips and the cold gray
eyes were all I'd ever really noticed before.

"What about Miss Wyndham?" I suggested,
thinking of the contrast between them.

He shook his head.

"Antoinette Wyndham never met life—much less
death—half-way." He hesitated, then added, "Till
now—when it's too late."

"Is it ever too late?"

"Yes, Dr. Fisher. A woman can't put love and kindliness and grace out of her life for fifty years, as Antoinette has done, and then try to pick it up again, without its turning to dust and ashes in her hands. And I'm very much afraid that Antoinette can't build her love for one nephew on the hopes and rights of his cousins without suffering for it."

"Has she a legal right," I asked, "to leave all that property to Richard Wyndham? Couldn't the rest of them contest?"

He shook his head deliberately.

"The property is hers unconditionally. Undue influence could not be proved; she made her will when the children were quite young, she has never changed it."

"It's a pity," I said, as we turned in the linden avenue between the carved-stone pineapple gateposts of the Eliot house. "I'm sorry about Gail. The others can manage. I suppose Richard will sell out and leave town, when he doesn't have to watch his interests here any longer."

"I hope so," said Judge Garth quietly. "He doesn't belong here. The successful Wyndhams have always been buccaneers—sometimes respectable, sometimes not. Richard should go to New York. Don't make the mistake, Dr. Fisher, that most people in town make about that young man. He's the Wyndham type. His aunt knows it. That's why she worships him."

"What about Gail? Isn't she the type?"

"Perhaps. She seems more like her mother to me."

"I never knew her."

I stopped the car behind Eliot Wyndham's sport roadster that was pulled up under the porte-cochère. "I'll leave the car here," I said. "I'm not staying long." Both of us got out.

Alice was in the drawing-room. All the Wyndhams were already there. I looked curiously around —not entirely suspecting, of course, the unpleasant scene that was to occur just then, still less that this was the second Belasco scene in the drama of Miss Nettie's murder; but acutely aware that such a luncheon was mere folly, and that I was a fool to have come to it. As it turned out, however, it was a good thing that I had come.

Old Miss Nettie, like an ancient witch almost, was seated in state in a high-backed chair near the fire. Her nephew Richard was on one side of her, Alice Penniman on the other. At sight of the malicious and crafty smile on the old woman's thin lips I became more uneasy than ever.

Alice nodded to me.

"How do you do, Judge Garth—so good of you to come! You know Miss Wyndham, of course. You've known her much longer than any of us!"

She wagged a roguish finger at him.

Judge Garth just isn't the sort of person to be playful with, but Alice is a great leveler. I must say they nearly all fall for it.

"Indeed he knows me," Miss Nettie spoke up promptly. The croak in her old voice reminded me of a hungry raven. "And he knows all my brothers' children."

Judge Garth acknowledged the greetings of the young people, and stepped to one side where Gail stood, ivory white and tense as a coiled spring. Her smoldering dark eyes moved from face to face in the room. The handkerchief in her hand was a tightly-rolled clenched ball.

She smiled at Judge Garth. Miss Nettie's beady black eyes glittered with animosity as she looked at the two.

"Certainly like her mother—isn't she, Tom?"

The girl's full lips tightened, but she remained outwardly composed. I wondered how much longer she would stand it.

"I think possibly she's even more beautiful than her mother, Nettie," replied Judge Garth, bowing slightly to Gail and turning back to the old woman.

I caught the look of battle in Nat Penniman's eye. He and his father were talking to Chase and Eliot Wyndham at the end of the room.

"I didn't know you thought anybody could be more beautiful than Gail Seaton, Tom Garth."

The old woman sniggered with such an unpleasant leer that I positively shuddered.

A faint smile warmed Judge Garth's gray marble face. He raised his hand and put it lightly on Gail's shoulders.

"Only her daughter, Nettie," he said.

The girl smiled gratefully. Suddenly she flushed, and her eyes, meeting her cousin Richard's, flashed angrily.

Miss Nettie's eyes darted from one to the other. Her lips closed menacingly; she sat bolt upright in her chair.

"She don't like you, Ricky," she croaked angrily. "Well, she don't have to. I'll take care of you, boy. She can look to her fine friends."

There was a dead silence in the room. The men at the other end stopped their talk abruptly. Alice Penniman was staring, fascinated, at her chief guest.

Richard Wyndham leaned down and took one of the scrawny brown talons in his hands, and patted it affectionately.

"Come, come, Aunt Nettie," he said coaxingly.

"I won't come, come! I know they want my money and my house—but they won't get it! I'll burn it down first. You'll get it, or I'll burn it down!"

Miss Nettie's hand shook, her eyes glinted from a face flushed with rage, her voice had risen to a scream of fury. Clutching her nephew's arm she pulled herself erect, planted her thorn stick on the rug, and glared around the room.

"Thinks her money will buy a Wyndham! It won't. She'll not get my house, that woman. I'll burn it, I'll burn it!"

The old woman had lashed herself into a passion. Her nephew tried to force her gently back into her chair. She pushed him savagely away. Gail stood white-lipped, her hands clenched tightly at her sides. Judge Garth stood beside her, his face a cold, imperturbable mask. Alice Penniman, her face white as chalk, lips blue, groped with one hand for her husband's arm, staring at the terrible old woman almost beside herself with fury.

"You!" Miss Nettie screamed. "You—devil! Trying to get me here to poison me! *I* know. Making love to my boy!"

Alice Penniman's left arm suddenly straightened out at her side. Her right hand clutched at her heart, and she fell forward, writhing with pain.

I rushed to her as quickly as I could.

"Water!" I said. "Nat, get my bag in the hall, on the table!"

Nat Penniman struggled to open the bag. I snatched it from him, opened it and got out the bottle of digitalin tablets I always carry. The cap stuck. When his unsteady hands twisted it off with a final jerk the tiny pellets flew out and went all over the floor. I picked up one that fell in my lap, put it on Alice Penniman's tongue. Gail held a glass of water to the fainting woman's blue icy lips, contorted with pain. I waited, my fingers on her pulse, until it strengthened.

"Get some very hot water, Gail, please," I said.

"Have them fix her bed. Lift her carefully, Sam, by the shoulders. Nat, you take her feet."

Together they carried her out into the hall and up the wide staircase. I followed them, wondering at the expression of horror I'd caught for a second on Miss Nettie's wrinkled malignant old face.

When I came downstairs, after getting Alice comfortable and in bed, Miss Nettie and her favorite nephew had disappeared. The others—Chase, Eliot and Gail—were still there.

"Did Richard put her up to that?" Chase Wyndham was asking.

"No," said Gail curtly. Her voice came in clipped, highly-charged gusts of sound. "I loathe him—but he wouldn't do that. She would. She hates all of us. She'd do anything to hurt—me. Oh, Mr. Penniman, I begged Mrs. Penniman not to ask her! I knew something would happen!"

The asbestos man leaned forward and patted the girl's arm.

"That's all right, Gail," he said. "We know how Mother is. She'll be all right to-morrow."

"But I *knew* something like this would happen!"

The girl clasped her hands together so tightly that the small fragile knuckles showed in white sharp ridges. "I've known it since she said they could put the tablet on the house."

Her full lips trembled. I thought for a moment that she was going to break down. But she took a sudden spasmodic breath, and turned to Judge

Garth, who had been sitting silently in a wing chair by the fire.

"What is it, Judge Garth?" she demanded urgently. "Why does she hate us so? I knew when she sent for me and said I'd have to stand on the steps with her, that she wasn't doing it because she wanted me there."

Judge Garth was silent for a moment, gazing into the fire that had been built for the old woman.

"Your aunt," he said judicially, weighing each word, it seemed, "is a woman of very violent passions. She was jealous of your mother. That turned to hatred—and although in a sense she won, in another she lost."

Somebody there may have understood him. I didn't.

"Does hatred last forever?" the girl cried passionately.

"Hate lives longer than love," said Judge Garth. "It feeds on itself, Gail."

Chase Wyndham, who had been sitting with his head bent in his cupped hands, looked up.

"Why take it out on me and Eliot, then?" he asked with a sardonic twist of his mouth. "I'll tell you, it makes me sore—and it isn't altogether greed either—to see that place go to Richard. My God, it's worth thousands. He'll turn it into a gambling joint."

"He'll sell it," said Gail tersely.

"That'll be a great help," Chase retorted. "That

place ought to bring a hundred thousand, without the furniture, even now. Three years ago we could have got two hundred thousand. I know. I was talking the other day to a museum fellow. He says he's had inquiries, dozens of 'em.''

Some days later I suddenly recalled the glance that passed between Nat Penniman and his father.

Eliot Wyndham broke in quietly.

"The place and the whole property will be Richard's,'' he said. "Why fret about it? Anyway, we must be going. I needn't tell you how sorry we are about this affair, Mr. Penniman. Judge Garth, can we take you down?''

Judge Garth shook his head.

"I'd prefer to walk, thank you," he said. "I need the exercise.''

While they were speaking Nat Penniman had edged over to me.

"Stay a while, will you? Dad wants to see you."

I nodded.

"How about you, Gail?'' Eliot said from the hall.

"No, thanks. I'll walk down with Judge Garth.''

The judge bowed.

"Very good of you, my dear. Good day, Mr. Penniman. Good day, Nat.''

He turned to me.

"You'll take care of this child, Dr. Fisher? We can depend on it. Good day to you, ma'am.''

Mr. Penniman came back to the fire and stood in front of it, his hands clasped behind his back.

"I declare, Ruth," he said to me, "I don't know what to make of it." He was genuinely worried.

"She'll be all right, Sam. Rest and quiet for a few days."

"It's not that—it's that damned old woman. Do you think she'd burn that house down?"

I shrugged. If Miss Nettie would burn the house and herself and all her works I'd consider it a boon to the town. Her warped, venomous personality hung over the whole place like a plague. Children never played on Charles Street. I've actually been called to the bedside of a hysterical youngster whose nurse had told her, "Old Miss Nettie'll get you!"

"She might," I said.

"Good riddance, if you hear me," said Nat. "Mother'd give up about it, Gail'd get a little peace. Between Mother and that old scarecrow she's afraid to call her soul her own."

"I'll try to get her to go away for a while," I said. "I want to see your mother before I go."

I started out into the hall.

"Will she need any more of these?"

Nat held up the tiny bottle that had been standing on the table.

"Not to-night," I said.

I was starting on upstairs when I was struck by the queer expression on his face.

"That's funny," he said.

"What is?"

"Why, I picked up nine of these things, off the floor. Or I thought I did."

I went back into the room. He held the bottle over to me. There were two of the tiny pills in it.

I smiled at the puzzled look on his face.

"Then you must have dropped them again," I said. "Did you put them in the bottle when you picked them up?"

"Sure," he said. "No, by George, I didn't. I just put them on the table."

"Then they got brushed off."

Nat bent down and looked under the table.

"Right you are, lady doctor," he said. "Here's one of 'em, anyway."

He turned up the edge of the rug.

"There must have been a dozen, altogether," he said. "Here's another. Oh well, they'll turn up in the vacuum cleaner."

But they didn't. Not in the vacuum cleaner.

CHAPTER

3

WHEN I came down from the Pennimans', shortly after three o'clock, Estaphine, my colored maid, greeted me at the door, her eyes like inverted white saucers with a dab of brown gravy in the center.

"Mistah Richuhd Wyndham, he telephone, Doctuh. He says ol' Miss Nettie's been took right bad and will yo' come roun' soon as yo' gets home."

I was as much astonished at that news as Estaphine was, but being of a superior race I was able to conceal my surprise.

"Very well," I said.

That wasn't enough for Estaphine. She followed me into my office and puttered about, moving chairs and wiping things off. I glanced over my engagement book and made a note of the state of Weems's twins' whooping cough.

"Ah sure hopes Miss Nettie ain' real sick," she said hopefully.

Considering the state she had left everyone at the Pennimans' in, I felt it wasn't likely. But I said nothing. Finally Estaphine came to the crux of the matter.

"'Deed an' Ah don' see why they done call us," she said, inquiringly. "They's always had Doctuh Cathcart when they sick. They say ol' Miss Nettie said many a time no woman doctuh couldn' neveh touch a yaller dawg with the mange if it was hers."

What Estaphine meant was that Miss Nettie didn't approve of women's practicing medicine, and that she'd never been a patient of mine. The odd part of it is, that Estaphine, like nearly everybody else in town, knew Miss Nettie's opinion on every possible subject, from the complaints about the spinach at Miss Sally's boarding house to the length—or lack of it—of the new first grade teacher's hair. And they're all unpleasant opinions. This in spite of the fact that Miss Nettie never went out but once a week when night was falling, and then only as far as the corner post-box; and saw only three or four old friends who came in Thursday for a glass of blackberry wine. That of course doesn't count Daphne Lake, who's been going there for the last two months at nine o'clock each morning to comb the old woman's hair, and it doesn't count the underground current of information that flows in and out of every kitchen in the South. But that old woman managed, some way, to be a figure, sinister and unrelenting, behind every lilac bush. For instance: she'd not been to church for seventeen years; yet last year they didn't give the miracle play because of Miss Nettie's remarks on the figure of the girl who'd played Anastasia the year before. It's incomprehensible to an outsider. Estaphine understands it perfectly.

When it became apparent to her that I didn't intend to discuss Miss Nettie's preference in physicians, she brought out the noon mail.

"These heah lettahs done come, Doctuh."

I glanced over them.

"This is for Miss Gail," I said, handing one back. "Put it on her table."

Estaphine took it and looked at it.

"This heah's one of them lettahs that done puts her in a state," she said calmly. She held it up to the light.

"What do you mean?" I asked. No one with sense will under-rate these old Negresses' power of observation.

"Ah means Miss Gail got one of 'em las' week while you was out. She turn like death, an' purty soon she run upstairs. She didn' come down to dinnah, and she didn't eat nothin' on the tray Ah sen' up."

That was something I hadn't heard about. Gail lives, as I've said, at my house, and has since she entered high school; but she's a reticent young person. I know very little of what goes on in her dark head. At dinner I see a pale ivory-faced girl through the flickering candle light. That anything of terror or fear was pursuing her, that her dark eyes concealed more than other normal twenty-year-old dark eyes concealed from the older people they live with, seemed inconceivable for a second. Then it seemed quite possible.

Estaphine never pursues a point once it's made. Now that I knew something was wrong with "Miss Gail," and that there was trouble ahead in the letter she held in her hand, the subject was instantly dropped. This time, as often, for something even more startling.

"Does yo' want a glass milk 'fore yo' goes out? Ah heahs yo' all didn' have no lunch at Mis' Penniman's."

I know small town telegraphy, or telepathy, or whatever it is, very well; but I was surprised at that.

"Mis' Penniman's shofer Alec done brought Miss Nettie down," she went on. "He say she was a-buzzin' an' a-cacklin' an' a-carryin' on like mad. She say she done teach 'em wheah they belongs. Alec say she say she bets them Pennimans done stole her coffee pot."

"What coffee pot, Estaphine?"

"Yo' 'members that ol' coffee pot somebody stole from Miss Nettie las' June? They say she done got three hundred dollahs fo' that coffee pot. From the insurance society."

I did remember it then, and was about to say so, when the telephone rang, and Estaphine tactfully disappeared. It was Richard Wyndham.

"I wanted to know if you got my message. My aunt's better. Nerves, I suppose; but if you'd come around, we'd be obliged to you."

"Doesn't Dr. Cathcart usually attend your aunt?" I asked.

He laughed.

"She won't have him in the house, Dr. Fisher. Insists on you."

"All right," I said. "I'll come in a few minutes."

It was a strange scene that I took part in that afternoon. When I got there the iron gates of the Wyndham house were closed again. A couple of dirty-faced kids peeking through the bars were the only indication that the day was different from others. One of the odd things about the place was that no children played in front of it, or climbed its walls to swipe the peaches and cherries that they could have reached. When I drove up the two youngsters scampered off, and I heard one of them say, "Jeez, the old dame must be sick!"

I pulled the bell. After a moment old John, bent almost double with age, came hobbling down the brick wall between the two giant magnolia trees and touched his cap. He opened the gates. I drove in much as Lafayette must have done a hundred years ago—except that my vehicle was faster and much more comfortable. I shouldn't be surprised, however, if old John had opened the gates for him too. He's the local Methuselah. I see his bent figure every day, hobbling down through the streets to the market, silent and sad, an old market basket on one arm, to do Miss Nettie's food. I've never seen him speak to anyone, but Estaphine says he's still as sharp as his mistress.

I turned up the old carriage drive and stopped in front of the porch. The bronze plaque looked garishly new against the deep yellow-brown and mauve glaze of the old bricks.

Richard Wyndham opened the front door for me.

"Good of you to come, Dr. Fisher," he said as our eyes met across the threshold. We stood there a second or so, definitely taking stock of each other. And somewhere in the short space of time that elapses between one's opening a door and inviting a person to enter, the subtle mocking smile in Richard Wyndham's eyes, and the ever-so-faint curl in his lips disappeared. I don't know when it was, although I must have seen it happening. All I know is that the man who opened the door and looked me straight in the eyes was the Richard Wyndham I knew slightly and had heard a good deal about. The man I followed through the hall into the small drawing-room to the left was different. The amused supercilious air was gone. There was something considerably more chilling in its place.

"No use apologizing for this noon," he said, pushing back the shutters so that a little more light could get in the dim musty room. "You know how my aunt is."

"I haven't seen your aunt for seventeen years, until to-day," I said, probably a little stiffly.

"Well, you didn't notice any change, did you?"

We seemed to get on a little better than I'd expected. It appeared that his aunt had come home very much upset.

"I think the morning was too much for her. After all, she's seventy-five years old. It's the first time in years she's seen anybody, except two or three old girls as old as she is. I told Gail it was a mistake to ask her to go to the Pennimans'. I'll tell you, Dr. Fisher, I think they asked for what they got. You can't expect my aunt to act like a monkey on a string."

There was just the slightest accent on the "my."

"I'm sure no one expected Miss Wyndham to act like a monkey on a string," I said coldly.

"I think they did," he said carelessly. "At any rate, Doctor, you can't say that Mrs. Penniman was entirely disinterested."

Of course that was true. I couldn't at any time say Alice Penniman was disinterested. Standing at that moment in the superb drawing-room of Wyndham House, under the eyes of Josiah Wyndham and his wife—portraits by Peale—appraising the room and each other from opposite walls, with a plump Miss Wyndham in yellow satin smiling skeptically down from the elaborately carved overmantel, it was doubly impossible. Richard Wyndham knew as well as I that Alice Penniman would have given her head for the Sheraton armchair I was standing by, or the Chippendale mirror between the windows, or the card table in the corner, or any other of those exquisite pieces, for that matter. No one of them had ever been in any other room, since the day they were made.

"I'd better see your aunt," I said. I thought it time to change the subject.

Richard's eyebrows went up a little.

"She's upstairs," he said. "Let me take your bag."

I followed him down the dark hall.

"She keeps the place black as pitch," he said when I knocked against a chair by the door opening into the stairway. "I've tried to get her to put in electricity. But she won't do it. The telephone's all I've managed."

I noticed suddenly that he had stopped in the hall, and looked back at him. He was looking down over the banister, his head bent a little to one side, listening intently.

I waited. He looked at me queerly.

"Did you hear something down there?" he asked.

"It's probably John," I said, surprised.

He shook his head.

"John stays in the wing," he said. "You wouldn't catch him in the cellar. He once saw Lafayette and my great-aunt Prue dancing down there."

He looked queerly at me, and bent over again, listening.

I suggested that probably it was a rat.

He nodded politely, unconvinced.

"I'll take you up," he said. "Then I'll just have a look down there. My aunt has lost several things lately. Anybody could get in this place."

It all seemed strange to me. I had heard something, or thought I had, and when we started up the stairs it seemed to me that it began again.

"It's probably just these steps," I said.

"Maybe," he said shortly. "My aunt's room is in back."

At that moment there came out towards us the trembling quaver of an old voice, through the far door on the right.

"Is that you, Ricky?"

He raised his voice. "Yes, Aunt Nettie. I'm bringing Dr. Fisher."

There was a silence. We went on down the hall and into the bedroom.

The old woman was lying, dressed, except for her bonnet, as she had been that morning, in an enormous four-poster with red and white figured canopy. How Alice Penniman would have loved that, I thought. Except for her sharp beady eyes she might have been a grotesquely arrayed mummy. The horrible little Mexican hairless bitch was drooling and panting beside her.

She raised herself on her pillows and motioned for me to come around beside her.

"I don't feel right," she piped in her high wavering voice. "If I'd eaten anything at that woman's place I'd know I'd been poisoned. That's what she was planning to do. I'm an old woman with one foot in the grave, but you can't fool me."

I took her hand and felt her pulse. It was rapid, irregular and weak, but hardly more so than usual in a woman of her years. She watched me like a hawk.

"Ricky," she ordered suddenly, "telephone for Tom Garth. I want him to come over here."

He looked up suddenly at her, and I caught his quick glance at me.

"Are you sure you want him, dear?" he said.

"Am I sure I want him!" she said mockingly, with a quick display of temper. "Yes, I'm sure! Don't try any monkey-shines on me, young man."

She turned back towards me.

"Even he's turning on me," she began querulously.

"Oh no, Miss Wyndham," I said. "He just was trying to be sure it wouldn't be too much for you to see anyone else to-day."

She gave a most unpleasant croaking laugh.

"Don't let him fool you. He thinks I'm going to change my will. He thinks I'm crazy enough to leave my house and my money to that hatchet-faced spawn. . . ."

I exercised the medical right of interruption. She was working herself into what Estaphine calls "a right bad state."

"Come, come!" I said. "Don't get excited. Where

can I get a glass? I want you to take a little medicine. Just a tonic."

It wasn't a tonic that I was thinking of, but
her pulse was fluttering, and the word "tonic" is
always comforting.

She pointed at the table to my left, half hidden
by the bed curtains. I'd entirely failed to see it in
the dingy half-light.

"If you don't mind, Miss Wyndham," I said,
"I'm going to open these shutters. We need a little
more light."

"Not too much," she said complainingly. "It
hurts my eyes."

I threw open the shutters and came back. On the
table by the bed was the greatest array of patent
medicine bottles that I'd ever seen, and I've seen
many arrays of them.

I pointed to one of them, a specific for all known
and some unknown diseases, compounded of herbs
and rattle-snake oil.

"What in Heaven's name do you have this stuff
for?" I asked.

"It helps John's rheumatism, and I reckoned it
ought to help mine," she whined.

Richard came back into the room.

She leaned forward eagerly, clutching at my arm
for support.

"Is he coming, Ricky?" she demanded.

"Said he'd be here in a couple of minutes, Aunty.
I'm going down now to let him in."

"I've known Tom Garth since we were babies," she said, turning back to me. "My people and his came here together before there was any United States. They were rich once, but they ain't any more."

"Judge Garth is a very fine man," I said. She seemed to be waiting for me to say something.

She laughed very unpleasantly.

"I'm not a fine woman, I suppose you mean. Well, if you believe that little minx you took in off the streets, you certainly don't think I'm fine."

I said, "You're wrong, Miss Wyndham, if you think Gail has ever said one word against you. And in my opinion, you treated her very badly."

"I didn't any such thing. She's got no claim on me. What was her mother, I'd like to know? Where'd my brother find her? I could tell you!"

She raised her old body and leaned closer to me, her eyes glittering venomously. Suddenly we both heard footsteps below us. She sank back, twisting her mouth into a toothless grin.

"It doesn't make any difference," she said.

We waited for her nephew to appear with the judge.

"I'm sorry to hear you're sick, Nettie," said Judge Garth quietly, coming up to the bed. They did not shake hands. They seemed to know each other too well, I thought, to make any such thing necessary.

Miss Wyndham nodded curtly at her nephew.

"Go out, Ricky," she said, "and shut the door. Here, wait a minute. You can take Fifi down and let her have her milk. Go with Ricky, baby."

She handed him the obscene beast.

"Fifi's eighteen," she said. "You remember when I got her, Tom?"

Judge Garth nodded. I can't think that he liked the hideous little animal any better than I did.

Old Miss Nettie was laughing to herself.

"He thinks I'm going to change my will. Maybe I'll do it. Even my Ricky's getting tired of an old woman."

Her voice had that unendurable nagging singsong.

Judge Garth said nothing until it was plain that she was going to continue her complaints. Then he interrupted.

"What did you want to see me about, Antoinette?" he said quietly.

She hesitated, stretched her hand over to where the dog had been, and began picking nervously at the counterpane.

"I'm feeling perfectly well," she snapped suddenly. "And if I weren't I wouldn't send for any woman to doctor me. I've got medicine enough and to spare without anybody giving me any more."

I got up to go, but she clutched suddenly at my arm.

"Then what do you want with Dr. Fisher and me?" Judge Garth repeated patiently.

"It's about something you said, Tom," she said suddenly and very unexpectedly as far as I was concerned. It was hard to follow the old woman's moods. They changed in a breath from a sort of savage intensity to the querulous whine of the old invalid.

"You said Pa would come back and curse me if I left everything to my Ricky. You said that, didn't you?"

She looked at him in mingled anger and fear, and I looked at him too, in a good deal of surprise.

Judge Garth's thin lips tightened.

"I said that, Antoinette," he replied sternly. "It is true. When your father made his will he told each of you that when the last child of his died, the property was to be divided equally between his grandchildren. He left a sacred trust. You have—so far —denied it."

There was something greatly moving in the quiet firm voice of the old judge, sitting erect and uncompromising on the side of the bed. Miss Wyndham moved uneasily.

"I know you think I'm hard, Tom," she said almost ingratiatingly. "But I've decided to do something for the girl. That's why I sent for you, and Dr. Fisher. I'm going to do something for her."

I was glad then that I had not followed my first impulse not to come, or my later impulse to leave. I moved forward a little. Judge Garth inclined his head gravely. I thought, however, that I noticed a watchful expression in his eyes.

"I'm glad to hear that, Antoinette," he said.

"Get me my will, Tom. It's in the bottom drawer there. It's on top. Do you see it?"

She was sitting up now, pointing excitedly while the judge followed her directions.

"Give it to me!" she cried.

He handed her the document. She opened it feverishly.

"Read it, there," she ordered. "About personal property. It says everything in the house goes to my nephew Richard. Doesn't it?"

Judge Garth took the will, and read aloud two paragraphs in which Miss Wyndham had willed and devised all her property real and personal to her nephew.

"You're going to change this, Nettie?" he said.

Her eyes snapped cunningly.

"No!" she said. "I'm not going to change it, but I'm going to give the girl something. You're my witnesses. I'm going to give the pearls to that girl. I'm going to give them now to Dr. Fisher to give to her. You're the witness. Then he won't get them."

Judge Garth shook his head. I saw, this time distinctly, the same alert and watchful look in his eyes.

"It would be better to put that in your will, Nettie."

"I won't make a new will."

"A codicil, then."

"I won't change it. I'm going to give them to her now."

I had hoped, of course, that she was actually going to make a more nearly equal division of the property. I'd never seen the pearls, but I didn't imagine they had any great value.

As if knowing just about what I was thinking, the old woman darted me one of her bright hungry glances.

"You'll take them for her?"

"I'll be very happy to do so, Miss Wyndham," I said.

"There!" she said. "You see? She's got more sense than you, Tom Garth! She's willing to take whatever she can get. Help me up."

I helped her get up and got her stick for her. She went with surprising agility to the highboy in the corner, and turned to beckon me.

"Come here, Dr. Fisher! They're in there, in that box. Get them out."

I opened the drawer, and took out a purple velvet box. She was greatly excited. She kept hopping about, tapping the floor with her stick, and talking almost incoherently about her various jewels.

I put the box on the table, and brought up a chair for her. Judge Garth stood silently beside us. She fumbled about with the little bunch of keys at her belt, and finally selected a tiny gold one. She started to put it in the lock, and stopped suddenly.

"Why!" she gasped. "It's not locked!"

She dropped the key on the table, snatched up the purple box with her shaking brown claws, and lifted the lid. The box was empty.

She stared at it a second, then turned an agonized face to Judge Garth.

"They're stolen, Tom! They're stolen!" she cried. "My pearls! They're gone! She's got them, she's stolen my pearls!"

"Who has stolen them?"

"That woman. That Penniman woman. She's got them. She got my coffee pot—they say she bought it, but it's just like mine that was stolen last March."

She sank back against the chair, her eyes staring straight ahead.

"Tell Ricky to call the police, Dr. Fisher."

Judge Garth stood motionless, looking steadily at her.

"You'd better have a look about, first," I said.

"No, no. They were there this morning, I tell you. I took them out. Call the police."

I looked inquiringly at Judge Garth. His stern old face was impassive. I hesitated a moment, then went out into the hall and looked around. There was no telephone in sight. I went downstairs. I saw none in the hall, but it was so dark there that I could hardly see anything. It seemed to me that I could hear someone in a room nearby, so I pushed open the door that led down into the hyphen that joins the main house and a wing that is—so far as I know —unused.

Richard Wyndham evidently didn't hear me; he did not look up. He was leaning over the stair railing, looking down at the top cellar steps. I could see his lower lip caught in his strong white teeth. I followed his gaze, and saw instantly what he was looking at. On the landing there were two marks, very easy to recognize. In that second he realized that I was there. He straightened up quickly, and as he did so stepped down and trampled on the two perfect small heel marks of grass and clay.

"Your aunt wants you to telephone the police, Mr. Wyndham," I said. "Her pearls have been stolen."

I could swear—in fact I did swear, later—that his face turned a shade paler.

"Thank you," he said. "I'll call them."

Then he smiled his old quick flashing smile.

"Your rat turned out to be a thief, Dr. Fisher. But he's got away. There's no one down there now."

I knew that Richard Wyndham was lying.

CHAPTER

4

I THOUGHT that neither Richard Wyndham nor his aunt seemed greatly concerned over the loss of the pearls. Fifi's wheezing, gasping return occupied the old woman's attention, and Richard, from all I could make out, regarded it as good riddance of bad rubbish. He did, however, call the local police.

"Not that it'll do any good," he said carelessly.

Judge Garth agreed to wait until the police came. I was already late at the hospital, and left as soon as I got my bag.

It was after five when I got home. Chase and Eliot Wyndham were holding a council of war in my living room. At least Chase was pacing the floor, gesticulating wildly. His brother was seated on the sofa, his hands thrust deep in his pockets.

He got up when I came in.

"I hope you don't mind our taking possession like this, Dr. Fisher," he said. "We're taking Gail out to dinner. She said you wouldn't mind our waiting here."

"Not at all," I said. "I expect you to come here. This is your cousin's home."

"That's awfully decent of you," Chase said angrily. "She ought to be living with our aunt."

"I don't think she'd like it very much. In fact, I've just come from there, and I'm sure she wouldn't."

"Not sick, is she?" Chase inquired hopefully.

"Not in the least. She called me over because she wanted to do something for Gail. She intends to give her the pearls."

Eliot looked rather pleased at that, but it didn't seem to me that Chase did. In fact he seemed to me to be more like his cousin Richard was reputed to be than anything else. He seemed chiefly interested in Chase Wyndham.

"The pearls, however," I went on before either of them could say anything, "have disappeared."

They stared at me, then looked sharply at each other. Chase laughed bitterly.

"I'm certainly the prize fall guy," he said. "You know, I'm the fellow that insisted on her getting all the stuff in the house insured, because a friend of mine at the Metropolitan told me it was worth pots of money. And you know who's been paying the premiums? Chase Wyndham, the half-wit. Me. Now, where do I stand?"

Eliot smiled.

"You knew she was leaving all of it to Richard,"

he said quietly. "I don't see that you've got any kick coming."

"Oh yeah?"

I could understand why Richard was not greatly cut up about the loss of the pearls. I was about to say so, when Estaphine came in with a message from Gail. "She say if yo' don' mind will yo' come upstairs a minute?"

The girl was in her room lying down. She had been crying. Her shoulders still heaved convulsively in sharp dry sobs.

I glanced about the room. She was still wearing the white wool dress. Her hat was thrown on her dressing table, and by it was an open typewritten letter.

She raised her head and saw my glance at it.

"Read it," she gasped, and buried her head in the pillow again.

I read the letter. At first I didn't understand it. When I read it the second time I understood it too well.

It was one of those cowardly anonymous attacks that insane people make on defenceless women. It happens most frequently in small towns, and it is not the product of a poisoned pen so much as of a poisoned mind. I read it again. It came from someone who knew the history of the Wyndham family.

"How many of these have you gotten, Gail?" I asked, sitting down by her bed.

She sat up and brushed her hair listlessly from her pale face.

"This is the third," she said dully. "The others said the same thing, except not anything about Nat Penniman."

"I wish you'd told me about them."

"Why? I didn't want you to know that anybody could say things like that about me and my mother. I was afraid maybe some of it was true, and I didn't want anybody to know it—especially you."

"My dear child," I said, "don't you know that this is something that happens every once in a while where there are people who are ingrowing? Usually they aren't responsible. You're not the only person this has happened to."

"That's what Judge Garth said," she replied. "I went to him with the second letter. He said it was someone in town, it had happened before."

"Have you shown him this?"

"I called him up. He said to tell you about it, and then burn it up and try to forget it."

Personally I much preferred keeping it and having a detective brought in to find out who had written it. And I said so.

"It oughtn't to be difficult. The number of actual enemies you and your aunt and family have in town must be fairly small."

She shook her head.

"If Judge Garth says to, I'd better burn it. I did the others."

"Do as you think best," I agreed. "But if this should happen again, you must leave it to me. It ought to be fairly simple to trace. It's written by someone who can't type very well, on an old machine. The spelling may be purposely illiterate, or not. The paper is cheap. There might even be fingerprints on it."

The girl shook her head hopelessly. I took the letter and envelope and went to the empty hearth. I struck a match and held it to a corner of the paper. When it was almost burned I dropped it into the grate and scattered the brittle charred flakes with the poker.

"There," I said. "That's better. You get up and take a bath. You'll feel better. Your cousins are waiting downstairs. Would you like Estaphine to get dinner for you here? I'm dining at the Pennimans'."

She got to her feet and managed a sick little smile.

"We were going to the hotel, but that would be better. I don't feel much like going out."

I nodded.

"I was at your aunt's this afternoon," I said, thinking she might be interested in the news that she'd hear very shortly anyway. "She sent for me and Judge Garth. She wanted to make you a present of her pearls."

With a flash of the true Wyndham spirit she whirled around, her eyes blazing.

"Did you tell her to keep her pearls and take them to the devil with her?" she cried. "I won't take a thing that belongs to her. I've told Judge Garth that, and I mean it."

"Well, you needn't worry," I replied. "They've disappeared. They weren't in the jewel box."

"Disappeared my hat," Gail answered rudely. "Along with the coffee pot last March and the ruby ring in June. Don't you think it's queer that things start disappearing from the Wyndham house now? They've never lost as much as a green plum for two hundred years."

She was standing with a flushed face and snapping eyes, looking too much like the rest of the family for my comfort. The writer of the burned letter in the fireplace, or anyone else, could tell me that Gail wasn't a Wyndham until he was black in the face, and I'd not believe him.

"What happened to them, then?"

"How should I know?" she replied indifferently. "All I know is that my cousin Richard manages to do very well for himself and that platinum blonde he drags around. You know that if anybody wanted to really steal anything, they'd go to the Pennimans and get something with a turn-in value."

"You don't actually think Richard's fool enough to run the risk of stealing something that will belong to him soon anyway. Do you?"

Gail shrugged her shoulders expressively.

"How do you know he'll get them?"

"I heard the will this afternoon."

"I know. How do you know she's not going to do what she said she would, and burn the place down some night? I wouldn't put it beyond her. Cousin Richard knows that as well as I do. I think he's wise to get what he can while he's got a chance. I would."

The cynicism of modern youth is very appealing.

"I thought you just said you wouldn't have a thing your aunt has."

"And I wouldn't," she flashed instantly. "I said if I were Richard I'd take what I could get. But I'm not—thank Heavens."

She started for the bath. I suppose she was really thinking "worse luck."

Estaphine met me at the foot of the stairs.

"Young lady to see you, Doctuh. She's in the office. Ah say it ain' youh hours, but she say she got to see you."

"Very well. Tell Mr. Chase and Mr. Eliot that they're having dinner here with Miss Gail."

"Yas'm."

"Make some spoon bread and bring them in a glass of sherry now."

"Yas'm."

My office is one of the side rooms downstairs. It can be entered from the outside by way of a small reception room, or through the front hall past the open door of the long living room where the Wyndhams were still at it. In fact the living room, din-

ing-room and office all open off the large hall at the
foot of the staircase. The office door is usually kept
closed unless Estaphine prefers to have it open. It
was half open now. I went in expecting to see
almost anyone but the "platinum blonde" whom
Gail had just been talking about.

"How do you do, Miss Lake," I said, closing the
door behind me.

She had changed from her white starched uniform, and had on a simple black crepe frock that
marvelously set off her white skin and the ripples of
shining hair showing under a small black hat. Her
face was a little flushed, and she had a sort of
breathless air that suggested either that she was in
a hurry or excited about something.

"I hope you'll excuse my bothering you," she
said. "The maid told me these weren't your hours,
but I . . ."

"That's quite all right," I interrupted. "Sit down.
Can I do something for you?"

She sat on the edge of the chair by my desk and
crossed her knees. It isn't an uncommon experience
for a person to come to a doctor on the impulse of
the moment and change her mind when actually
face to face across the corner of a desk. She hesitated several seconds, and I waited. At last she
raised her head with a sudden little smiling gesture,
and looked me straight in the eyes.

"This will seem perfectly absurd to you, Dr.
Fisher," she said, and swallowed something that

seemed to have got in her throat. "But you know I've been going over to Miss Wyndham's two or three times a week to rub her head and comb her hair?"

I nodded. Everybody in town knew it.

"Well, you see, she's got rather fond of me, or something, and to-day—this afternoon when I got back to the shop—there was a message there for me, saying she wanted me to come and spend the night with her."

"Yes," I said, concealing my surprise as well as I could. "Are you going?"

I couldn't think of anything else to say.

I thought the girl stiffened a little. Her voice certainly was a little metal-edged, and she spoke more rapidly.

"Yes, Dr. Fisher. I'm going."

She smiled suddenly. She has really a remarkably intelligent face, with moods in it that vary as abruptly as Gail's, although of a very different type. Gail's face has an intensity and subtlety that this girl's hasn't, but there is something delightful about the open and closed effect of Daphne Lake's expressions. It's brilliant sunshine one moment, and the next a cool common-sense sobriety that tones everything down at once.

"The absurd part of it is that I—well, I just wanted somebody to know I was there, and why I was going . . . so that if anything happened . . ."

The smile faded again.

"Do you expect something to happen?" I asked, smiling at her serious lovely face that even a lot of ridiculous make-up couldn't make hard or unintelligent.

I noticed that curious quick metallic quality in her voice again.

"Not really," she said. "Only such odd things have happened all day that I feel . . . a little uneasy."

"Then why do you go, Miss Lake?" I asked, very reasonably.

"I've got to. I couldn't not, you see, after she asked me. It's . . . well, it's important."

"My phone number is 350," I said, writing it down on a slip of paper. "If you're alarmed, call me. I'll come around. I think you're plucky to go at all."

She got up, her breath coming a little faster than it should. I think she was rather more frightened than she liked to admit. I thought too there was something else she would have liked to tell me. She hesitated a moment, then put out her hand impulsively.

"Thanks very much, Dr. Fisher. I hope you don't mind. I'll feel better, with you . . . knowing."

"Be sure and call me. I'll be here after nine. Good luck."

She moved to the door of the reception room, and stopped.

"Oh, by the way, Dr. Fisher—I came in the front door. Isn't that Eliot Wyndham in there?"

"Yes."

"Is he one of these Wyndhams?"

"He's the younger son of Miss Wyndham's second brother. Would you like to meet him?"

"Oh no, no," she replied hastily. "I just wondered if he was. He doesn't look much like them."

She smiled and put out her hand.

"Thanks again, Dr. Fisher. I'll go out this way, if you don't mind. It's nearer."

It wasn't, of course; in fact, it was considerably farther. But I understood her. Obviously, I thought, Daphne Lake and Eliot Wyndham had recognized each other, and Daphne clearly, for some reason, did not want to renew their acquaintance. Just then, however, I was much more concerned with the thought of that girl's spending a night behind the dark shuttered windows of Wyndham House, than I was with any possible past in which Eliot Wyndham figured. An old woman, an old darkey, an old dog, weren't the company I'd choose for Daphne Lake.

At the same time I couldn't forget the little heel prints on the cellar landing that Richard Wyndham had so neatly obliterated when I came suddenly on him bending over, looking at them. Why I simply assumed they were Daphne Lake's, without even thinking why I thought so, I don't know.

It all goes to show how many of our judgments

are influenced by a whole background of knowledge and hearsay and unfounded assumption. I assumed that those heel marks were Daphne's because in the first place they were a woman's, and a stylish woman's at that. I took it for granted that Daphne Lake's heel marks were the only ones that Richard Wyndham would want to conceal. And so on. My opinion wasn't influenced in the slightest when I came out of my office to join the Wyndhams for a cocktail and met Estaphine taking a pair of high-heeled pumps she had just cleaned up to Gail's room.

And to cap the climax, I hadn't at that time remotely connected any of it with the actual disappearance of Miss Nettie's locally famous pearls.

CHAPTER

5

I CAME down the hospital steps about nine o'clock, a little uneasy about the burning pain in old Miss Adams's stomach, and very uneasy indeed about young Daphne Lake alone in Wyndham House with Miss Nettie, her dreadful senile little dog, and old John. Just what I was afraid of I don't know. Physically Daphne was more than a match for all three—even supposing they meant the girl any harm, which I didn't think for a moment was true. I don't believe in ghosts, so it wouldn't be Lafayette, Washington or Josiah Wyndham that made me almost shudder at the idea of her being there. There was some evil aura about those dark musty rooms with their elaborate and beautiful cornices and carved woodwork, and all their treasures in pictures and furniture. It should have been clean and lovely. It wasn't. In some way it was terrible, repulsive. Like its owner and her dog—not like Daphne Lake.

I turned my car down Liberty Street and left into Charles Street down near the water. The walled garden of Wyndham House was on the left. Driving over to the right I could see the dark roof of the house across the black silent peaks of the giant magnolias. I stopped in front of the gate and peered in. The white window trim outlined the dark shuttered windows. There wasn't a light visible through a single chink in the closed blinds. There wasn't a soul stirring there. Yet the house had that ominous sense of life, a soft of marked vitality that kept it from being a sleeping peaceful mansion in a lovely garden.

Somehow, sitting there, I seemed to have a feeling of someone moving in the house, silently, stealthily, from room to room. Something awful, unclean. I shook myself abruptly to my senses. I needed a rest, obviously. Bermuda. Even New York would do it. I realized unhappily that I was becoming as morbidly imaginative as half my patients.

"Sleep will do it," I assured myself. But at the same time I felt a very great reluctance to leave the spot where I was. However, there was no point in my staying there; and the Thornton twins might decide to appear any moment, fifteen minutes out from town. I put my foot on the starter and put the car into gear. As I did so I heard a car behind me, and looked around. The car had come along Front Street and had parked at the end of Charles Street near the wicket in the wall of Wyndham House, about three hundred feet behind me.

I thought at first that it was an indiscreet young couple stopping by the water, and started to go on my way, when a very odd thing happened. The cowl lights of the car went on and off, on and off. I caught their flash in the mirror over my windshield. They flashed again twice, this time in quick succession. Then the car was dark. I turned off my engine. The next moment I clearly heard a grating noise close by. I leaned my head out of the car window, and saw the shutter in the upper right-hand window of Wyndham House swing slowly open, and a tiny flame appear. It burned an instant and went out, appeared again and vanished. If there was a human figure behind it, I couldn't see it.

I started my engine and let the car go slowly forward. My lights were still off. Under the shadow of the great full-foliaged elms across the street I thought I could get to the corner without being seen. Just why I thought it any of my business to find out who was in the car down by the wicket, I'm not sure. But I did. I slipped around the corner to the left, into Chase Street, turned on my lights and stepped on the gas. I was around the block and into Front Street within two minutes; but I was too late. I saw the red tail light of the other car turning the corner of Chase Street, and when I got there it was gone. I hadn't even got close enough to be sure it had a Maryland license.

That incident had the excellent effect of clearing the cobwebs out of my brain. If whatever danger there was in that house could open a shutter and flash a signal in answer to another signal from a waiting car, then it wasn't as intangible or subtle as I'd feared. Nevertheless, I left my car parked in the drive when I got home.

Estaphine had left a light supper on the table in front of the living room fireplace. I poured myself a cup of steaming bouillon and ate a sandwich while I glanced through the evening papers. The cat came in and settled himself sociably in a chair across the room, and there we sat until I heard the clock on the stairs strike a deliberate and sonorous eleven. The Thornton twins, I thought, had decided to wait till to-morrow, and Daphne Lake was still all right, and I was getting sleepier by the minute.

It was exactly twelve o'clock when the phone by my bed rang. I woke with the Thorntons on my mind. They had been there longer than Daphne Lake.

"Hello," I said.

"Dr. Fisher! There's something in the house! Can you come quickly?"

The terrified whisper at the other end of the line brought me sharply to my feet.

"I'll be there," I said, and slammed up the phone. Why we didn't call the police I don't know. We both took it for granted that I would be enough, and yet I didn't even take my bag with me. I only took the big flash-light I keep in the pocket of the car. And I'm not sure yet how I got over the garden wall, not being as young as I once was, except that I drove the car on the sidewalk down on Front

Street, close to the wall, climbed from the top of it
onto the wall and jumped.

I picked myself up, hoping the best for my ankle,
and ran up the path across the lawn to the front
door. Daphne Lake was huddled inside it. She was
fully dressed, and her hair was still as neatly coiled
as ever. Her face was white as a plaster, her firm
young jaw set bravely. Still the hand she put on my
arm with a warning gesture was trembling.

I turned the radiant beam of my lamp into the
pitch darkness of the wide hall.

"I'll go first, let me take it," she whispered.

I shook my head and stepped over to the closed
door on the left. This was the room where Richard
Wyndham had received me. I flung it open and
turned my light into it. I felt Daphne start and give
a little gasp. I turned quickly.

"Nothing, just the picture there. I thought it
moved! I'm really sunk!"

The slightly amused eyes of the early Wyndhams
watched us a little mockingly, perhaps, but they had
not moved, even under such a sudden attack.

We closed the door and crossed the hall. The
library was empty. No one had been in it for years,
it seemed to say. From there we went into the long
room at the back. I tried the door by the fireplace.

"That's a blind door," Daphne whispered. "It
doesn't open. Miss Wyndham told me so."

We went upstairs. Each step creaked a warning
that we were coming. The brilliant beam of my

light picked out nothing but a Sheraton chair and a Newport grandfather clock on the landing.

We advanced cautiously into the room in which I had seen the shutter opened.

"I'm sleeping here," she whispered.

I looked at her sideways. The light threw deep shadows up into her eyes. Her round set chin came into sudden relief.

I glanced at the mahogany dressing table. Beside her brush and comb was a flattened package of cigarettes; beside it a lighter. I was about to ask her directly what it was all about, when a dull far-off sound brought both of us rigidly alert.

She clutched my arm.

"That's it! It comes up there!"

She pointed to the fireplace. I turned my light on it. It was empty and cold.

"It must come from the cellar," I said.

The girl shuddered, and grasped my arm with a grip of steel. That reassured me. She wasn't falling out yet.

The noise came up the brick chimney again, this time less heavy, as if someone were scratching about down there.

Suddenly an idea came to me that had been in the back of my head since the middle of the afternoon.

"Where's Miss Wyndham's room?" I whispered.

"In there, but we don't want to wake her up."

I paid no attention to her, but walking as noiselessly as I could approached the old woman's door and listened. There was no sound in the house except the even tick-tock, tick-tock of the old clock, and still that spasmodic scratching in the chimney.

I turned the brass knob of the great lock and felt it give. I opened the door and peered into the inky blackness of the big room. There was no sound; it was as silent as the grave. Slowly I brought the door back again to close it, when I suddenly remembered the dog. I pushed the door open again and stepped into Miss Nettie's bedroom. And I instantly knew that someone else was there, someone I've met too often not to sense and know almost by instinct.

Death was in Miss Wyndham's room, standing in the corner, waiting for us to come.

I turned my light on the great four-poster bed. There was Miss Nettie, her head lolling to one side against a mountain of pillows, horribly, offensively dead.

I gave Daphne my light and stepped to the bed. One stiff arm in a long flannel sleeve stretched out towards me. I lifted it, though there was no need. It was cold; rigor had already set in.

Daphne stood beside me, her eyes dilated in horror. The hand holding the lamp shook violently. I took it away from her and moved the beam slowly around the room and back to the bed.

Then I saw the terrible thing.

On the other side of the old woman, caught in the fold of the enormous linen sheet, was the bitch. Her teeth were bared, her rheumy eyes staring, her thin legs stretching up from her fat old body. She was dead too. Then I noticed, on the table beside the bed, an overturned glass.

I took in the scene with one glance and drew the sheet up over the old woman. Sometimes death is beautiful. It is when it comes as rest after a long life of happiness or even pain. But it wasn't here. On this scene was stamped nothing but revenge and hate.

"Let's get out of here," I said sharply to Daphne.

She turned slowly and half stumbled out of the room. I closed the door, locked it, and put the key in my pocket.

"Now," I said, "I'm going to see what's downstairs." I really felt more confident, now that I knew what I was dealing with. "You'd better stay here."

"No. I'll come with you."

"Then pull yourself together."

We went slowly and softly as we could down the stairs and out into the hyphen where I'd seen Richard Wyndham that afternoon examining the heel marks on the floor.

The doors that let down over the steps were still open, as they had been then. I turned my lamp on the dark hole of the cellar. I thought it was clear that those doors were not usually open. At least not both sections. One side had no cobwebs; on the other there were hundreds, torn roughly asunder and hanging in dust-laden festoons along the gray stone foundations.

With my shaft of light ahead of me I went down
those stairs, Daphne following. It was cold down
there, and damp. The great brick-and-stone wine
cellars and chimney shaft loomed up at our side.
We stopped and listened. There was nothing but
our breathing, and the faint drip of a trickle of
water somewhere. Unless—and I felt Daphne's
body stiffen—that was the sound of someone else's
breathing around the pillar. I moved cautiously
along it, with my light ahead of me. I heard a sound
then, plainly. I stepped forward more courageously
than I felt, heard the sound again, and swung the
beam of light sharply to my left, just in time to
catch the sight of the heavy stick crashing swiftly
down on my arm, with a sudden wave of pain that
relaxed every muscle in it and sent my lamp flying
off into the corner.

The switch struck as it fell. We were left in that
poisonous black void.

There was the sudden dash of someone running
lightly. We heard the doors of the cellar steps crash
down. My arm hurt like fire. I crawled forward on
the cold sodden earth to find my lamp, and heard a
soft thud behind me.

That wretched girl had fainted.

CHAPTER

6

FORTUNATELY Daphne Lake recovered without very much effort.

"Did you see who that was?" she asked, getting to her feet. She was shaky but game.

"I didn't. Did you?"

She didn't answer, which at the time didn't seem remarkable. Instead she took the flash-light out of my good hand, and holding the beam down, stepped cautiously around the huge pillar of masonry that supports the great chimneys of Wyndham House.

"I wonder what he was doing?" she remarked casually, if a little weakly. I must say that at the moment I wasn't very much interested. My arm hurt like poison, but it wasn't broken, although not much use for the time. Also, I was thinking of the grim occupant of that great dark room upstairs. We should have called the coroner before we came down here, I thought, wondering at the same time if our unknown friend with the stick had locked the cellar doors. If so we might be in for a long stay.

Daphne came back with the light.

"There doesn't seem to be anything unusual

there," she announced in her normal voice. "Let's
see if we can get out."

I suppose I should have suspected something from
the perfectly natural way in which this girl with the
peroxide hair and keen eyes and painted lips took
the whole affair for granted. Now that she'd got
hold of herself, she didn't seem to mind being shut
up in perfectly foul cellars with cobwebs heavy with
dust and dirt catching her hair and face. In fact, she
seemed to get a certain amount of satisfaction out
of it.

The cellar doors were not locked. Daphne pushed
them up. We came out into the comparatively clean
air of the hyphen.

"We'd better wake John first and get the gates
unlocked so the coroner can get in," I began, and
stopped at the queer expression in the girl's face.

"Coroner?" she said incredulously. "What do
you want him for? Can't you make out a certificate?"

Our eyes met for an instant in the deceptive
shadows cast by my light. I shook my head.

"I'm not here professionally," I said. "Furthermore, I've never treated Miss Wyndham. I
shouldn't care to make out a certificate anyway.
Not under the circumstances."

"What do you mean?" she demanded, staring at
me with a frown.

"Just that. Do you know where John sleeps?"

She nodded without speaking. Then she began impulsively.

"Listen, Dr. Fisher . . ."

I stopped her at once.

"My dear," I said, "I don't like any of this. The thing we certainly must do is get Dr. Michaels—he's the coroner—here. Let him decide what to do."

"But I don't understand you. What's to be decided? The old woman's dead—why all the bother?"

"Because, Miss Lake, it's not only the old woman that's dead. The dog is dead too. I don't believe in coincidences. Not with that glass turned over on the table. This is Dr. Michaels's affair. Not mine."

She became suddenly very quiet.

"I see," she said. "I'll get John. He sleeps in the other wing. There are some lamps on the big dining-room. The phone's in there too."

In a few moments she came back to the big room where I was standing, looking around me in the feeble but very encouraging light from the old oil lamp in the center of a gorgeous Phyfe banquet table.

"He's coming. What do we do now?"

"We wait right here until he comes," I replied. "Did you tell John she was dead?"

She nodded.

"I don't think he understood it, though. I told him you were here and you wanted the gates opened."

She sat down abruptly and put her elbows on the table, and sat there, chin in hands, staring into the light, saying nothing. I watched her out of the corner of my eye.

"This is all pretty funny, isn't it?" she said finally, without looking at me.

"There's Dr. Michaels," I said, hearing a car. "We'll see if it is."

She got up, switched on my flash again, and started to let him in.

As she went out through the carved door into the dark hall she turned back and said, "It's funny whether he says so or not."

Dr. Michaels and I stood looking at each other across the wide expanse of Miss Nettie's great four-poster. His eyes were narrowed and calculating.

"You didn't need me to tell you this old woman's dead, eh, Dr. Fisher?" he asked satirically.

"No," I said. "I needed you to tell me what she died of."

"Heart, of course. Good God, she's eighty if she's a day. Look at her."

"I don't want to look at her. I thought it was heart too. Of course there's the dog."

"Sure. You often read about that kind of thing. Dog lived with old woman, dies on the grave. Not uncommon."

I was in a curious dilemma. I thought of Gail and the girl downstairs. Miss Nettie meant nothing to me. On the other hand, I didn't particularly care about being accessory after the fact. What's more, while Dr. Michaels is a decent enough sort of person, he's not the sort I'd care to have know that I willingly winked at a lapse of justice. Especially when it involved a person as closely connected with me as Gail Wyndham.

"Isn't that right, eh, Doctor?" he demanded.

I shook my head slowly.

"No," I said. "You'll have to explain that overturned glass to me."

He turned around as if he hadn't noticed the glass before. I focused my flash on it, making a shaft of brilliant light through the dim semi-darkness made by the oil lamp on the table at the foot of the bed.

The water from the glass had dried. A thin white film stained the polished mahogany surface of the table.

Dr. Michaels turned back to me. His face was a little flushed. I remembered the rumor that he'd been grooming Richard Wyndham for mayor, and I remembered that the coroner is one of the boys.

"There's no use being hasty about this, now, Dr. Fisher," he said.

"No indeed," I agreed pointedly. "You're quite right. That would be a mistake."

He hesitated.

"Perhaps I'd better see Judge Garth about it."

I couldn't imagine Judge Garth making compromises with justice. I made one myself, therefore, by saying, "What about Mr. Taylor?"

Mr. Taylor is the State's Attorney. Sound but not fanatical.

"We'll see," he said. He reached down and covered the figure on the bed.

"In that case," I went on, "I'm going home. I called Richard Wyndham. He didn't seem to be home. Somebody ought to get in touch with him. It's not fair to leave that old Negro here alone with her. He'd be dead himself in the morning, if we did."

Dr. Michaels grunted. He doesn't care much about Negroes.

"I'll call Mr. Wyndham again, if you want me to, Dr. Fisher."

We both started. I had not heard Daphne Lake come into the room.

"Please do," I said. "I'll be down in a minute."

Dr. Michaels's eye followed the lithe figure of the girl to the door. He nodded significantly.

"What's *she* doing here?"

My arm was aching badly and I was getting tired of all this.

"I'd leave that to the State's Attorney if I were you," I said. "Your job's much simpler. Good night."

He moved forward in a hurry at that. I didn't blame him much for not wanting to stay there all alone. But Richard Wyndham was his friend, not mine. I felt he could stay for him as well as I could.

He handed me the lamp, which I held while he locked the door. Then he turned around and said, with a calculating nod, "I'm mighty afraid we're letting ourselves in for something."

I didn't say anything.

"You and I may not like to think it, Dr. Fisher, but that looks like murder."

He dug me in the ribs with his elbow.

Nat Penniman's comment in such cases is "You're telling me." I refrained, however.

Instead I said, "Do you really think so?"

"I'm mighty afraid so," he returned soberly.

Downstairs Daphne was waiting, sitting curiously deflated and hollow-chested, in the big dining-room.

"He's coming right over," she said dully.

Dr. Michaels spoke up briskly.

"Then I'll be seeing you in the morning, Dr. Fisher."

And while I was trying to get Daphne to stir herself, he got away and left us there.

She looked unhappily at me.

"I wish you'd go home, Dr. Fisher," she said. "I'll stay until Richard comes. Then I'll go home too. Old John's out there sitting on the steps. I'll be all right."

"Would you prefer to see Richard Wyndham

alone, Miss Lake?" I said as kindly as I could, being entirely at sea in the matter.

She shook her head that was snow-white in the dim light.

"No. I don't want to see him alone. In fact I'd rather not see him at all."

Then she added a queer remark. In fact I was quite getting used to her abrupt introductions of new points of view.

"All this is his now, isn't it?"

"I suppose it is," I answered. "Except the pearls. But since they're gone, I suppose they're his too. I mean, he gets the money they're insured for."

"Why? Weren't they to be his too?"

"His aunt sent for me and Judge Garth this afternoon to give them to me for Gail. That's when she found they were gone."

She looked at me with a frown deepening between her arched brows.

"You mean she asked you to come here this afternoon, and then found out the pearls were gone?"

I nodded.

"I'm sorry," I said. "I hate to see Gail get absolutely nothing."

"She doesn't really rate anything," the girl said calmly.

"What?" I said.

"She's never been so swell to Miss Wyndham."

"I think she's been as decent as her aunt would let her be."

"I wonder," she returned coolly. "Miss Wyndham showed me a letter her niece wrote her. It wasn't very pleasant. Unless you like blackmail."

I stared at her in horror.

"What are you talking about?" I cried. I could hardly believe my ears.

She shrugged her slim shoulders nonchalantly.

"It's you that called the coroner, Dr. Fisher," she said. "I hope you like it. *I* think you'd better have let well enough alone."

I was still thinking about that when Richard Wyndham appeared in the front door. Daphne didn't look up. He stood there looking from one of us to the other.

"Miss Lake says my aunt has died, Dr. Fisher," he said coolly. "I can't pretend to be sorry, so please don't expect me to. Do I have to see her?"

"No," I said. "You don't have to see her."

Half an hour earlier I might have been surprised at this display of callousness. After what Daphne Lake had just said hardly anything could surprise me.

He seemed, however, to think I hadn't understood him.

"I want to make it clear to you," he went on, "that of course I hated my aunt intensely. All this was a job. The pay was pretty good."

He glanced up at the magnificent carved cornice, and let his eye fall insolently on the pair of sunburst tables against the wall.

"Not so bad, not so bad!" he said quietly.

Daphne Lake stood up abruptly, her fists clenched at her sides, her brown eyes blazing with anger.

"Stop it!" she said in a low voice. "Haven't you any decency? You don't deserve to touch a brick of this place. You're all alike, you're all rotten! Every one of you!"

She turned, and in a second was out of the room. I heard her swift sharp heels on the brick walk until suddenly there was silence.

I looked at Richard. His face was pale and his jaw set.

Then I picked up my lamp.

"Did you know, Mr. Wyndham," I said quietly, "that there may be some question about your aunt's death?"

He answered me almost absent-mindedly, as if he was thinking intensely about some remote matter.

"Question?"

"Yes. I believe Dr. Michaels said there was some possibility that she was murdered."

With that I left too.

CHAPTER

7

IT was the next morning that my interview with Judge Garth took place, in his office at the court-house.

"Mr. Taylor will handle this thing," he said slowly, moving his heavy swivel chair back from his desk and getting up. "I needn't say, Dr. Fisher, that it will be necessary for you to give the authorities all the evidence in your possession."

The evidence of a bruised arm in a sling and Dr. Wilkins taking my patients until I could use it comfortably again, I could hardly suppress. I wasn't so sure about the rest of it.

"Does that include the letters Gail has been getting, Judge Garth?" I asked, and met his cold, impersonal scrutiny.

"If they would seem to be pertinent to her aunt's death, Dr. Fisher, yes."

After a pause he added, "It was my understanding that she had destroyed those letters."

"She has," I said, "except for one. It came this morning. I have it here. Would you like to see it? It says . . ."

He raised his hand, quickly.

"If you believe it is germane to the case, it will be your duty to see that it is put into Mr. Taylor's hands," he said sternly. "It would be highly irregular for me to pass on any possible evidence before the case is tried. Keep it, Dr. Fisher. I trust to your honesty . . . and discretion."

I put the letter in my bag, and looked covertly at him. Was it possible that the uncompromising old man was advising me to destroy the letter? His lean gray face was like a rock. Nothing in it or in his cold eyes moved.

We sat in silence for a moment. Then it seemed that his face became a little less frigid, and he said, almost gently, "Don't misunderstand me, Dr. Fisher. Your profession and mine are similar and different, at the same time. Your job in this case is done. Mine has just begun. Personal considerations cannot come into it. You have been very honest; Dr. Michaels told me he would not have thought it murder if you hadn't pointed it out to him."

I winced a little.

"I'm afraid I thought it was a duty, Judge Garth."

"And it was. And it was more than that. When you have seen as much crime as I have, Dr. Fisher, you'll realize how much of it is brought to light by just such a fortuitous happening. It forces one to believe in something higher and more intelligent than chance in the conduct of the universe."

The idea of myself as an instrument of destiny was a little disconcerting, especially in view of my feeling towards Miss Wyndham. She seemed rather an odd person for a higher power to go out of its way to avenge. She had, in my opinion, caused enough sorrow in her own day, without now continuing it after her death. And I was responsible for it.

"Antoinette Wyndham was an unhappy woman, Dr. Fisher," Judge Garth was saying.

He was looking out of the office window, where the blue-bottle fly was still buzzing ferociously over his head, with his long lean fingers clasped loosely behind his old-fashioned frock coat.

"I used to believe that people were free agents, that they were responsible for what they did. I've sent men to the gallows because I thought that. I still think it, for some people. Antoinette was not one of them. She was driven by something outside of herself. Or inside; it doesn't matter. The Greeks had a word for it."

He glanced aside at me.

"You smile, Dr. Fisher," he said, naïvely. "You call it something else in medicine. The Greeks called it the Erinyes, the Furies. They drove Antoinette. Jealousy, despair, hatred, whatever it was. I've decided, in the last few years, that she was not responsible."

"Then what about the person who murdered her?

Is . . . he, or she . . . responsible? Shall you send him to the gallows?"

The softness had gone out of the old face. I saw again the cold, implacable jurist that everyone knew.

"He is responsible, Dr. Fisher. Your being there, and pointing out that there was murder, is evidence enough. Justice must proceed."

Usually I wouldn't agree. I did agree when he said it. His fine face earnest with conviction and determination convinced me. While we still have men like Judge Garth on the bench, I thought, there is hope for the soundness of our courts.

I wasn't, however, so sure about that when I went down the Court House steps, clustered with three-fourths of the local white unemployed male population of our town, awaiting jury service, chewing tobacco and discussing old Miss Nettie's death. The rumor that she had been murdered wasn't out yet.

It was fifteen minutes later.

The first good effect of Miss Nettie's death that I noticed was that it was a powerful tonic to Alice Penniman. Dr. Wilkins called, in my place, and she refused to see him. Her car was at my door when I got home. Alice, still pale but surprisingly controlled, was in my living room. It shows the power of mind over matter.

"You'll kill yourself some day," I said casually, moving the cigarettes away to where she couldn't reach them. Not that I regard tobacco as the sole cause of her pseudoangina. It comes from a number of things—her age, her emotional instability, her utter conviction that she can't stand strain of any sort, and chiefly her inveterate addiction to poisonously strong coffee and tea, which she drinks—or used to drink—continuously during her waking hours.

"And if I did," she said, "you'd send me some young pup just out of medical school to bury me. I was disgusted this morning. Cora brought my breakfast and told me Miss Nettie was dead. Samuel [Samuel is the asbestos husband] rushed in to stop her. He thought I'd have another attack. My dear, you don't know how it bucked me up. I mean, I'm terribly sorry, and so on—now you know that, don't you, Ruth?"

"Oh yes," I said soberly.

"Of course, you know how I *do* feel. After all, she was the last of the old aristocracy that managed to hang on to their own places."

"Judge Garth," I suggested amiably.

"Don't be provoking, Ruth. You know dear Judge Garth is different."

Alice has her own yardstick. I've never been able to find out what she bases any of her uniquely personal estimates of people on.

"Then this Dr. Wilkins comes in, says you've been out half the night and hadn't any sleep and broke your arm, and expects me to sit and listen to him. Now tell me what happened. I suppose a cigarette would be bad for me?"

"It would," I said. "And my arm isn't broken, and I wasn't out half the night, I was out all of it."

"Well, I knew you were somewhere, and I guessed it was Wyndham House. What's it actually like, Ruth? Do you think Richard will sell it right away? You know, I think, if I could get in there first. . . . Now stop it, Ruth. Don't be stupid. You know I'd like to buy a few things for Gail. After all, they're really hers, by rights—and do you know, Nat's going to marry her."

"Is he?" I said.

"Don't pretend you didn't know it. I think it's too bad, she didn't even get her share of the things in the house. But I'm going to talk to Richard. I think he'll see the justice of it."

I could see him listening to her. Still, she usually does manage to get what she wants, by hook or crook.

She hurtled on.

"Ruth, you haven't told me about Miss Nettie. How did you happen to go over there?"

"She sent for me. She wanted to give her pearls to me to give Gail."

"No!"

"But they were gone. Somebody had stolen them."

Alice can be consecutive enough when she chooses. She's not half the fool she sounds.

"That's odd, isn't it?" she demanded.

I nodded.

"Did Richard know she was going to give them to Gail?"

"I think not. She said he didn't."

"It's very funny, Ruth," she said with a queer look, "the number of things that have disappeared out of that house. First the coffee pot. That was worth about $500. I saw one exactly like it in *Antiques* for a thousand. That girl Richard runs around with showed it to me when she was doing my hair one day. She said, 'Did you see this?' I said, 'Yes.' She said, 'Miss Wyndham has one just like it.' And the next week it was gone."

"You don't think Miss Lake took it, Alice?"

Alice Penniman raised her carefully tended brows.

"I don't think anything. But that wasn't—now I think of it—the first thing that went. A ruby pin disappeared first. That wasn't very valuable. It was insured for about two hundred and fifty. Then the diamond ring set with pearls. Oh, then there was a pearl locket and earrings. They were all before the coffee pot."

"Miss Lake wasn't here, then, however."

"No, but Mr. Richard Wyndham knew her before she came here."

There was some triumph in her voice.

"How do you know?"

"He got her the job at Miss Chew's. I don't think that, I know it. Miss Chew told me."

"You oughtn't to believe everything you're told, Alice," I said.

"Well, we'll see about it. But I'll tell you one thing. I'm going to get those pearls for Gail if it's the last thing I ever do."

Her very determined blue eyes fixed on mine, daring me to make any more objections.

"You have my permission," I said. "Meanwhile you might like to know that it appears that Miss Nettie was murdered. Poisoned."

She took it with remarkable calm.

"I'm not surprised," she said, nodding her head. "Not in the least. Was it Chase, or Eliot? I wouldn't put it beyond either of them. Although I can't see what they've got to get out of it."

Which turned out a little later to be a very pointed remark.

"I shouldn't put it beyond Chase," I observed. "Eliot is rather different."

She shook her head vigorously.

"Not a bit. He's a wolf in sheep's clothing. One of your mealy-mouthed professors that don't fool me an instant."

"It doesn't matter, really," I said. "It's going to be awfully unpleasant for Gail."

"Nonsense, how can you say such a thing? If it wasn't one of them it was Richard and that girl.

There's your phone. If it's Samuel tell him I'm feeling fine and I've just left."

Alice's attitude towards her husband was half disdain and three-fourths obedience.

She was staring thoughtfully into the empty fireplace when I came back. Planning her campaign, I suspected.

"Samuel?"

I shook my head.

"If I tell you, will you keep it to yourself?"

"If you say so."

Oddly enough, I knew I could trust her.

"It was Dr. Michaels. He called up to tell me that they've tested the film of powder left on the table by Miss Nettie's bed. A glass of water was tipped over. When it dried the powder was left on the surface."

"Yes?" she said.

She was a little tense. I thought I'd been rather foolish to begin. Still, she'd be bound to hear it sooner or later.

"It was digitalin," I said.

There was a silence, punctuated only by the clock in the hall.

"What does that mean, Ruth?" she asked queerly.

"It probably means that both Miss Wyndham and the dog were poisoned by digitalin. They're examining her stomach to-day."

"Digitalin," she repeated thoughtfully. "That's what I take for my heart, isn't it?"

I nodded.

"I think I'll rest a minute," she said quietly. "Then I'd better go home."

Fifteen minutes later she drew on her gloves and stood up.

"I'm going now, Ruth," she said with a wan imitation of her usual brisk assurance. "I can think of so many things this might mean that I'm convinced it's something nobody's even thought of yet. That's the way things usually work out."

"Don't worry about it," I said, going with her to the door. "Just because they were your pills is no reason you should feel responsible at all. We'll probably find the missing ones under a rug or a cushion."

It was a perfectly asinine thing to have said, but the idea that she hadn't really heard about it never occurred to me.

She looked at me blankly.

"The missing ones?"

Of course, when she looked that way, I realized that she had known nothing about the tablets falling out on the floor, after that disastrous luncheon party.

When I explained it to her she only said, "Oh, I didn't know about that."

Then after a pause she added, "That makes it different, doesn't it?"

I went into my office, when she'd gone, and locked the door. Face to face with a dilemma of my own making, I didn't quite know which way to turn.

I took the letter addressed to Gail Wyndham out of my pocket and put it down on my blotting pad. This is what I had done. I had got home a little after three, bathed my bruised arm, and taken a couple of codeine tablets to relieve the pain. I'd got a little sleep, but was wide awake at seven, and was up and dressed when Estaphine brought my breakfast at half-past seven. I was downstairs at eight o'clock when the postman brought the mail. In it was a typed envelope addressed to Gail. I recognized it as another of those cowardly poisonous things she'd got before. The type and envelope were unmistakable.

Knowing what had happened the night before, and realizing that Gail would be in for a hard week or so, I put the thing aside and sent the rest of her mail up with Estaphine when she went to bring down her breakfast tray.

I seriously doubted the wisdom of Judge Garth's advice to destroy those letters. It seemed to me they should be traced and the writer punished; it's foolish to tolerate such a menace in a small community. I was, of course, keenly aware of what it would mean to Gail to have all this exposed unless it was done discreetly. At any rate, there was no point in upsetting her now, and I opened the letter myself—

the flap was loosely gummed. And this is what I read.

"Your theft of your aunt's pearls is known to two persons, one of whom is your aunt. You have hidden them in the cellar behind a loose brick in the foundation.

"It is also known that you tried to poison Miss Wyndham at luncheon at Mrs. Penniman's house and that you failed because I warned her in advance that such were someone's intentions without mentioning your name. She knows there is such a plot however and has confided in me."

So far I read, and stopped. The possibilities of such a thing had not occurred to me. Daphne's outburst I had discounted because of the nervous strain she was under. It was simply too ghastly to believe. My first impulse was to burn the letter, my second to show it to Gail and let her know what someone thought; my third to take it to Judge Garth.

And I had gone to him in his Court House office with that intention; but he was thinking about Miss Nettie, not her niece. Thus I was home again with the letter still in my possession, and Judge Garth's admonition about my honesty and discretion still in my ears.

I heard Gail's steps overhead, decided that obviously she couldn't have gone to the Pennimans', and made up my mind. I gummed down the flap of the envelope again, took it out into the hall and put it with several other letters on the table. Estaphine would take it up in a moment, or Gail would get it when she came down. If she were guilty, she would

burn the letter. If innocent, she would take it to
Judge Garth or bring it to me.

I came back to my office and sat down, trying to
make some sense out of the events of the last few
days, and was still sitting there when I heard a
light step on the polished stairs, and heard Gail
stop at the hall table. I heard the sharp tearing of
paper. It seemed a very long time before I heard a
movement followed by a light rap at my door.

"Thank God!" I thought, with a tremendous
flood of relief. "She's innocent, she's coming to tell
me.—Come in," I called.

She came in, beautifully self-possessed, all the
tenseness and terror of the last two days wiped out
as if by magic.

"Good morning, Aunt Ruth," she said. "What's
the matter with your arm?"

"I hurt it," I said.

"You've been cranking your car. Well, I hope it
isn't painful, but I know it is. Estaphine tells me
Aunt Nettie died. Too bad."

"Yes," I said, and waited for her to go on.

"I'm going up to the Pennimans', and then I'm
lunching with Chase and Eliot at one. Chase'll be
frightfully sore about all this. He actually thought
he could win her over."

She shrugged her shoulders and pulled on her
gloves.

"Anything I can do for you?"

"Not a thing, Gail."

"Then good-by. See you later."

When she'd gone, I went out into the hall to see if she could possibly not have got that letter. It was gone. So I guessed she had.

CHAPTER

8

THE news that old Miss Nettie had been murdered in her bed and her jewels stolen spread through the town like wildfire. Little knots of men gathered in front of the Court House and fire hall discussed it, making up missing facts as they went. Women in the market and over back fences wagged heads and tongues. In a short time bits of half-forgotten gossip were revived as indisputable fact.

Everyone took it for granted that it was a conspiracy between Gail Wyndham and her two cousins. Only a few seemed bright enough to see that they had nothing to gain.

"They'd not do murder so their cousin'd get all of it, sooner than was natural," said our mail carrier to Estaphine when she took the noon mail. "It ain't human nature."

"Deed'n thas so," she remarked admiringly. His profound observation was relayed to me in the following terms: "They tell me, Doctuh, that Mistuh Chase an' his brothuh wouldn' a done that 'cause Mistuh Richuhd, he goin' get the money—they ain'."

Nevertheless Chase and Eliot were obviously looked on with a growing sullen animosity. After all, they were foreigners, in the sense that they'd left the town and gone to New York to live. When they came back, this happened. The old lady had her faults, but they had no call to murder her.

So volatile and unpredictable are the emotions that move knots of idle men that Mr. Weems Taylor, the State's Attorney, telephoned me shortly after one o'clock and suggested that Gail stay inside for the time being. I said I'd call the Pennimans and tell her, also that I'd be glad to have Chase and Eliot move over to my house if he felt it might be unpleasant for them at the hotel.

By nightfall, all the wicked and unkind things old Miss Nettie had done in her long life in the town were forgotten. They forgot the winter before when she evicted a woman with a two-weeks' old baby whose husband had left her, because she couldn't pay the rent on one of the little brick houses in Kent Street. They forgot the poison she'd put on top of the garden wall for the stray cats who courted there. All her meanness and stinginess were forgotten, with all the absentee tyranny she'd exercised in a town where she owned most of the property of any value. After all, they said, she never came out, she didn't know what went on.

They even forgot the time Mr. Watts's bank failed, ruining dozens of prosperous merchants, and all the people whose savings were snugly tucked

away there—from the Negroes' Christmas Savings
Fund to old paralytic Mrs. French's meager monthly
income. An anonymous letter, never traced, started
the rumor that Mr. Watts was keeping a mistress in
Richmond and that that was where everybody's
money was going. Miss Nettie heard it first and
sent Richard to draw out her entire cash deposit—
around $5,000—and bank it in Baltimore. A run
started; it was over in two hours. Mr. Watts is still
paying off his obligations, Miss Nettie's money is
still idle in Baltimore.

But nobody remembered any of that. I even heard
a neighbor of mine speak of the wretched little
hideous animal as if it were a Borzoi.

Mr. Taylor came to see me in the middle of the
afternoon. He's a short heavy man with iron gray
hair and a manner in fitting with his situation. He's
a good politician, but I think fairly honest.

"I don't like the looks of this," he said. "Feeling's running pretty high downtown. Good God,
you'd think they'd be glad she's cashed in."

He mopped his damp forehead with a large
pongee handkerchief and stuck it into his pocket.

"There's a lot of rumors, Dr. Fisher," he said
next, "about that luncheon at the Pennimans'. I
understand it didn't go so well."

"No, it didn't," I agreed sardonically. "Miss
Wyndham was in a bad temper. She accused Mrs.
Penniman of trying to poison her so she could get
the house."

"I hear Mrs. Penniman had a heart attack then?"

"Mrs. Penniman is subject to what's called pseudoangina pectoris," I explained. "Any bad nervous or emotional strain will send her off, just as in true angina."

He nodded.

"I understand Miss Wyndham threatened to burn the house down."

"Yes."

"She'd have done it, probably?"

"Are you asking me?"

"Well, Doctor," he said, "I just wondered if you got the idea she meant it."

I shrugged my shoulders.

"You knew her as well as I do. She'd have done it, under the right conditions, I think. I don't know anything that would have stopped her."

Mr. Taylor hunched forward a little in his chair and fixed his green-gray eyes on me.

"Dr. Fisher," he said, "I understand that when Mrs. Penniman had that heart attack, you gave her a tablet or pill. That's right, isn't it?"

"Yes. Digitalin. It revives the heart. It's one of the commonest of the heart remedies."

"It's also a heart poison, isn't it?"

"Yes. It can be."

"Now, Dr. Fisher. I understand that when you gave Mrs. Penniman her medicine, several tablets spilled on the floor, and when you people left, they weren't all found."

"You got that from Judge Garth, I suppose," I said.

He smiled.

"I got some of it from young Penniman, some from the colored servants, and some from Richard Wyndham."

"Well," I said, "it's right."

"You see the point," he went on, "as well as I do. Miss Wyndham was poisoned with digitalin. There's not much doubt about it, though we haven't got the analysis yet. We've got the analysis on the dog. In fact, there's no doubt about it. Now, I'm not wasting any time—I can't afford to. What I want to know is this: was there enough poison in those tablets that weren't found to kill Miss Wyndham?"

"I don't know how many weren't found, Mr. Taylor," I said.

"You had how many to begin with?" he asked quietly.

"Exactly a dozen."

"Then there were seven missing, Dr. Fisher. Two were found on the floor after they spilled out. You gave her one; there were two more left in the bottle. Seven tablets."

"That would be enough," I said, "or more than enough. It depends on the state of the person taking them. A very small dose has been known to kill a person. Other persons have recovered from a large dose. There was more than enough to kill Miss

Wyndham. However—aren't you taking something for granted . . .?"

He broke in quickly.

"I know what you mean."

"Digitalin is not a hard drug to get. Any doctor keeps it. For instance, I have enough here to kill a hundred Miss Wyndhams. Many invalids probably have it on hand. Dr. Cathcart may even have prescribed it to Miss Wyndham herself—she had nearly everything else on her table."

He nodded and made a note of something. Then he looked up briskly.

"I understand that, Dr. Fisher," he said soberly. "But these two things together are very convincing. Coincidences simply don't happen that way. To all intents and purposes, that luncheon narrows down the obvious suspects."

"I think motive and opportunity are rather more important," I said.

He looked at me with a bland smile, and completely ignored my remark.

"I've asked the two Wyndhams to stay with you here until this quiets down," he said. "They ought to be here any time now."

He leaned back in his chair then, put the tips of his fingers together, and regarded me with a look of quiet persistence and determination.

"Dr. Fisher," he began with a little of his best manner when cross-examining a fairly intelligent witness, "you and I know what Miss Wyndham was like. We know that she made things as difficult as possible for her niece."

I added, "And for everybody else."

"Quite so. Now then, Dr. Fisher. I believe she called you over there yesterday afternoon. What for?"

"Mr. Taylor," I said with a smile, "you know very well why I went over there. Everyone in town does. Why not get down to it, and ask me what you really want to know?"

He accepted the thrust good-naturedly.

"I want to know how many hours you spent at Miss Wyndham's yesterday."

"Half-past three to half-past four, I imagine, and from quarter-past twelve to half-past two this morning."

"Who else was there at that time?"

"Richard Wyndham and Judge Garth in the afternoon, besides Miss Nettie, of course. Daphne Lake, and later Richard, in the morning."

"That's what I'm getting at. Where were Gail Wyndham and her two cousins?"

"That I don't know. They were here at half-past four when I came home. I think they had dinner here. They were out—at least the two men were—when I got home that night at nine o'clock."

"And Miss Gail?"

"I don't know," I repeated. "I was in this room until soon after eleven. I assumed she was upstairs. I didn't inquire."

He nodded.

"I see. Now, how about this Miss Lake? What was she doing there last night?"

"She came to see me about half-past six to tell me that she was spending the night with Miss Wyndham at Miss Wyndham's request. I think she was a little alarmed, and naturally so—at staying in that house all night. She wanted someone to know about it."

That didn't sound very convincing to Mr. Taylor.

"And she telephoned you about midnight?"

"Yes. Someone was in the house. My arm here is evidence of that."

"Miss Lake told me you had a mix-up with somebody in the cellar. She said at that time you'd already discovered Miss Wyndham was dead."

"Yes."

"Has it occurred to you, Dr. Fisher, that Miss Lake already knew Miss Wyndham was dead when she telephoned you?"

I thought about it.

"No, Mr. Taylor, it hasn't."

"Then I suggest it now. What do you think of it?"

"I think it's perfectly absurd."

"Do you also think Miss Lake didn't know who it was in the cellar, or why he was there?"

"I think she didn't know," I replied.

He thought for a moment.

"We haven't mentioned the pearls, Dr. Fisher," he said then. "Or the other articles of jewelry that have disappeared from Wyndham House from time to time during the last year."

It struck me for the first time that there was a definite motive behind all this jumping about.

"You haven't any reason to believe that those articles are in this house?"

"That's ridiculous!" I said sharply. "I suppose you mean Gail. To the best of my knowledge she hasn't been near that place for years, until yesterday."

"Then you've never taken the antagonism between her and her aunt seriously?"

"Not that way."

"You didn't give Miss Wyndham the digitalin yourself, by the way, Dr. Fisher?"

I shook my head and tried not to look surprised.

"What possible motive would I have?" I said.

"Miss Gail," he said. "Practically your ward. You're a close friend of Mrs. Penniman's. It would be a good thing for the community at large. I guess I could whip up a motive."

I shook my head again, and he smiled suddenly.

"Mr. Taylor," I said, "I'm afraid I'm not as altruistic as you think."

The next morning Roy Abbott, who's a teller in the Kent Savings Bank and one of Gail's most faithful followers, appeared at my office doorstep with a troubled face, turning his hat nervously in his hands.

"Thought I'd better come and see you on my way to the bank, Doctor," he began uncomfortably. "You see . . . well, it's like this."

"Sit down, Roy," I said, "and let's have it. What's on your mind?"

"It's about night before last," he said, still with some embarrassment. "I was looking out of my window—you know we live next to Judge Garth across the street from the Wyndham House."

I smiled at that, for I know very well where he lived. His mother is hypochondriac, and I spent my first six years of practice calling there once or twice a week.

"Well, I saw your car out in front of Miss Wyndham's."

He stopped and looked at me as if he had said all that was necessary.

"Well?" I said patiently.

"Well, you see, that was around nine o'clock. I saw you turn out your lights, and I saw the other car at the end of the road, and that funny light upstairs in Miss Wyndham's. You know, it looked like a signal."

While I felt that all this was distinctly unfortunate, I wasn't much surprised. People in small towns have a way of happening to see things. Roy was waiting for me to understand his difficulty, which I refused to do.

"Well, Roy," I said, "what about it?"

"Well, yesterday afternoon Mother said there was a man around asking if any of us had seen a suspicious looking person around there the day before."

I nodded sympathetically.

"Did you tell him about the car and the light?"

"I wasn't in, and I hadn't told Mother about it—she'd have had a fit. But you see, if Taylor gets on my trail . . . I mean, what I came here for was to find out what I was to say."

It's odd how evading the law has become second nature to young people. The police isn't an agency that you help any more.

"I'd tell Mr. Taylor everything you saw, Roy," I said. "I didn't tell him about it because he didn't ask me. By the way, did you recognize the other car?"

He hesitated.

"I thought it had a New York license," he said reluctantly. "But I wasn't sure. I don't want to get Gail in trouble, or her cousins either."

"Don't worry about that."

"But everybody in town's saying they did it."

"You don't believe that, do you?" I asked.

"I don't know what to believe, Dr. Fisher."

"Well, you'd better tell Mr. Taylor just what you saw. I'll speak to Gail about it to-day."

After he'd gone I sent Estaphine up to tell Chase Wyndham that I wanted to speak to him as soon as possible. He came down almost at once, and lounged nonchalantly into my living room.

"Look here, Chase," I said, having decided it was best to give up the attempt to distinguish the Mr. Wyndhams, "the other night I saw a car at the end of Charles Street by the water, signaling someone in Wyndham House. I've said nothing about it to anyone, but it seems that I wasn't the only person who saw it. Mr. Taylor is going to hear about it to-day."

Chase Wyndham regarded me with a slightly raised brow and a sardonic smile that would have done credit to his cousin Richard. He characteristically brushed an imaginary speck off his immaculate gray jacket, strolled over to the fireplace, and tossed his cigarette into the grate.

"May I presume to ask why you think that concerns me, Doctor?" he inquired coolly.

It was a question that, when I came to think of it, I found a little hard to answer definitely.

"The car had a New York license," I said. "I think the assumption is that it was your car. Still, as you can no doubt prove it wasn't, I suppose there's nothing to interest you in the matter. By the way, what time did Gail come in that evening?"

"Come in?" he said. "I wasn't aware that she was out. Eliot and I left here about nine o'clock. Gail was tired and said she was going to bed."

I couldn't, of course, be sure that Chase was not telling me the truth about the car. I was perfectly sure, however, that Gail had not been in the house when I got home that evening. Just how I knew that I can't say now, except that I did. I found myself very definitely hesitating about asking Gail where she'd been. I had the uncomfortable feeling that she'd say, or at any rate feel, that it wasn't any of my business.

I was thinking that over in my mind when I first learned of an event that very considerably changed all my speculations—and indeed those of everybody else—about this whole strange matter. Mr. Davis, Miss Wyndham's last attorney—she changed them twice a year—called me up to tell me, strictly between ourselves, that they'd searched high and low in Wyndham House, but had not been able to find Miss Wyndham's will. The box in the drawer in which it was always kept was empty; and it was nowhere else to be found.

CHAPTER

9

THE disappearance of Miss Nettie's will changed the whole situation in a way that is easily apparent. Unless the will were found, or another in its place, it meant that the old woman had died intestate. If that was so, her property would be divided equally between her niece, Gail, and her three nephews, Richard, Chase and Eliot. And a motive for the murder would be established that would be hard to get around.

It's odd how totally insignificant things become important in light of something else. It really isn't, of course, I suppose, because few things are ever significant except in their relation to something else. As I sat at my desk thinking of the possibilities of this new complication, I remembered hearing not long ago that Chase Wyndham's business was very shaky, and that he'd applied to his aunt for $10,000 which was enough to see him through. At that time it was a foregone conclusion that she'd refused him, although nobody actually seemed to know what she'd done about it.

Remembering Chase's handsome nonchalance, I

began to wonder if it didn't have a trace of very definite smug self-satisfaction that it had lacked at the Pennimans' luncheon. I doubted very much that Chase had any stern moral principle that would keep him from saving himself from ruin if the opportunity rose. In other words, I didn't think that Chase Wyndham would hesitate five minutes to do away with his aunt if he thought it would do him good and that he could get away with it. Up to this time I had refused to think of him as implicated strongly, for the simple reason that I didn't see what he had to gain. With Miss Nettie's will out of the way, he had a quarter share of at least $250,000 to gain.

Richard Wyndham, on the other hand, was the loser by something like $190,000. In my opinion, that let Richard completely out of the picture. I wondered how he was taking it.

I was turning that over in my mind when the front door opened. I heard Gail ask Estaphine if I was in, then a light tap at my door. She came in.

"Hullo," she said, sitting down on the edge of my desk and regarding me with serious eyes.

"Hello," I returned. "I thought Mr. Taylor told you to stay up at the Pennimans'."

"I couldn't. I just heard that they can't find Aunt Nettie's will. Do you suppose that's true?"

"I don't know, Gail. It makes a lot of difference, doesn't it?"

She sat staring intently with unseeing eyes at a

spot on the rug. Her clear smooth forehead was puckered and her mouth set tightly. I looked at her, wondering when this young woman had taken the place of the simple wide-eyed child I'd taken under my wing six years before.

"Yes, it makes a lot of difference, Aunt Ruth," she replied softly. "I've been trying not to think too much about it. Because it mightn't be true, and that would be worse."

"If you're going to marry Nat, it won't make that much difference," I said.

She didn't smile.

"I don't know that I'm going to marry Nat. That's Mrs. Penniman's idea, now that my aunt is dead."

I glanced up in mild surprise at the bitterness in the girl's voice.

"Last year Nat wanted to marry me and she wouldn't have it. Now it seems to be different. But I wasn't thinking of myself as much as Chase and Eliot—they always sound like a brand of coffee, don't they?—It makes so much difference to them that it's almost terrifying. If Chase gets fifty thousand, he can save his business."

"So Chase *has* been thinking about it," I reflected.

"He said he'd spoken to a man in New York who said the house ought to sell for about a hundred thousand even now. The furniture will bring fifty to a hundred thousand. Just think of the people he employs, and what keeping their jobs means to them and their families."

Chase, I thought, had been painting a very sympathetic picture of himself.

"But it's Eliot that I'd like best to see get it."

"Eliot?" I said. I was really surprised at that.

"Yes. He's been working for five years on a marvelous something or other to cure infantile paralysis. He thinks he's almost got it, Aunt Ruth, and he doesn't want to have to turn it over to somebody else. If he gets this money he can take a year off from teaching and finish it."

I must admit some astonishment at the high ideals of the brothers Wyndham. I always had regarded Eliot as a very sweet but pokey young man with a purely academic interest in chemistry. I was almost prepared now for Gail to tell me that Richard needed money to open a home for the aged and infirm.

It seemed to be a very serious matter to Gail.

"Nat said it was just that that was too bad about everything," she added, frowning unhappily.

"What was?"

"Well, he said that as my aunt was murdered, they'd be suspected as soon as anybody found the will was gone and they needed money. Nat said it simply stood to reason that they did it."

Seeing how serious it really was, I refrained from making any adverse comment about Nat.

"It sounds a little reasonable, doesn't it?" I said.

"Maybe they won't find it out—Mr. Taylor, I mean."

"I wouldn't figure on that, my dear," I said. "I'm afraid that's just the sort of thing Mr. Taylor will find out. If he hasn't already. It's his job, and he's nobody's fool. If a thing looks obvious to Nat Penniman, you can make up your mind that Mr. Taylor thought of it ages ago."

"I suppose that's right," she agreed. "He's coming here this afternoon. He wants to know where I was that night, when Aunt died."

I waited, hoping she'd say where she had been without my asking her.

"I was home here, but nobody can prove it," she went on.

"The important thing is that nobody can disprove it, Gail," I said.

Her velvety brown eyes sharpened suddenly, and looked very much like her aunt's.

"You don't think Chase and Eliot are mixed up in this, do you, Aunt Ruth?" she demanded suddenly.

"I don't know," I said. "They both had motive. They were both at Mrs. Penniman's when the pills went all over the floor. If they can prove that they didn't have the opportunity of dissolving them in Miss Wyndham's water tumbler between two and ten that night, and that neither of them had the chance to take her will after Judge Garth and I examined it, I think they're safe enough."

She leaned forward intently.

"But if they can't prove that?"

I shrugged my shoulders.

"Is that true of me too?" she said.

"I'm afraid it is, Gail."

She slipped suddenly down from my desk.

"Then I think I'd better see Chase a minute," she said quietly.

At that moment we heard Estaphine opening the door. The color drained from Gail's face and neck.

"That's Mr. Taylor now," she whispered. "I met him going up to the Pennimans' when I was coming down."

She stopped short and listened. Through the door we heard Estaphine say she would call Mr. Chase.

"Don't tell him I'm here, Aunt Ruth," she whispered. "Please! Not until I've seen Eliot or Chase."

Without waiting for me to speak, she went quickly out through the reception room.

I closed the outside door quietly behind her.

I heard Estaphine come downstairs and grumble something to Mr. Taylor. Then I heard him ask if I was in and if he could see me. Estaphine had been sorely tried by the number of odd people coming in and out all day for me, for no apparent reason, and said the doctor was in but it was inconvenient for her to see anybody.

With that I got up and went out into the hall.

Mr. Taylor was standing there with another man,

so obviously a detective, I thought, that it was a little funny. At least I've never seen anyone else with such a new light gray felt hat and an air at once keen, belligerent and ill at ease.

"Dr. Fisher," said Mr. Taylor, "this is Lieutenant Kelly, from Baltimore. He's in charge of this Wyndham case from now on. I've told him what you told me, and I've suggested that he keep in touch with you in case anything comes up and he needs your help."

Which I thought was a very good way of putting it, inasmuch as I had the three leading suspects under my roof.

Lieutenant Kelly and I took stock of each other. My first impression of him was that he had a job to do and by God he was going to do it and try to stop him. And, as a matter of fact, after he once became entirely convinced that I'd had no hand in the murder of Miss Nettie or the theft of her will, we got on very well. Well enough, in fact, so that when he finally packed to leave, he assured me, when we shook hands, that I had a friend in him whenever he needed one. "All you got to do, Doc," he said earnestly, "is just call Lieutenant Joseph Kelly at the Division of Detectives in Baltimore, and I'll be with you." I never figured out just what he expected me to do, but as he remarked so many times that week, "You just never can tell about people. It's funny."

It is funny. And if I ever did something in his

line of business, I'd be very glad to have Lieutenant
Joseph Kelly on my side. As will become apparent,
he was a much nicer, and very much shrewder, man
than would have been thought from his general
Sunday-suited, automobile-mechanic manner and
appearance.

Lieutenant Kelly, Mr. Taylor went on to explain,
was a person of distinction and considerable power.
He named several cases in which the criminal had
been brought swiftly to justice single-handed. For
the first few minutes I wondered if the State's Attorney was impressing me. Then I discovered that
he was—as Nat Penniman says—greasing Lieutenant Kelly. And after some minutes of this, during
which Chase Wyndham came in, was introduced,
and had the situation explained to him, Mr. Taylor
excused himself. He had, it appeared, some important paper work to do. By the relieved expression on
his face I knew that he was much pleased to be able
to pass the buck, as it were, to Lieutenant Kelly.
After all, Mr. Taylor is a politician. He could be
hard-boiled when the time came; but until that time
he much preferred to be everybody's friend.

Lieutenant Kelly got down to business at once.

"If you don't mind the Doctor's staying, Mr.
Wyndham," he said very affably, "I'd like to have
her. Now let's just check up on all this," he continued after Chase, who obviously didn't think so at
all, had declared it an excellent idea. "Just where
were you Wednesday night?"

"I dined here with my cousin and my brother," Chase said readily. "Then we drove out to Stonehill, where we lived when we were kids, and sat on the front porch. We talked and smoked, and had a drink, until pretty near midnight."

I couldn't help looking at Lieutenant Kelly, who at the same time glanced at me with a sardonic squint. His eyes were a greenish-brown, with hundreds of tiny wrinkles around them that deepened into a perfect maze when he was under the stress of any emotion. I thought now that he seemed a little annoyed that anybody would pick such a peculiarly unlikely story—gag, he called all such—to tell him. It sounded very arcadian, even to me.

"Well," he said philosophically, "I guess if you was trying to frame an alibi, you could do a better one than that?"

Chase nodded with a quick smile.

"Nice night?" asked Lieutenant Kelly.

"A beautiful night," said Chase calmly.

"You and your brother went out there?"

"Yes."

"Well, that's fine, now. I guess I can check that up easy enough. The owner saw you, I guess."

Chase shook his head.

"No," he said, "I don't think anybody saw us. The owners spend the fall in New York. In fact, I was talking to old Baker last Monday before I came down here. There are a couple of things in the attic

out there that belonged to my parents. Baker gave
me the key and said to get them."

"You after them that night?"

"No. We were just out there talking about things.
I don't see my brother often. We just wanted to
have a look at the old place by moonlight."

"Perhaps the caretaker saw you," suggested Lieutenant Kelly hopefully.

"Isn't any," said Chase.

"Well, that's too bad, isn't it? You know we got
to check up on all you people. Not that we don't
believe you, Mr. Wyndham, of course. Just rou-
tine."

Chase shrugged his shoulders.

"You can check up on it easily enough, Lieutenant," he said. "You'll find plenty of cigarette
butts around on the porch, and you'll find a flask
behind the hedge. I tossed it there when we were
leaving."

That seemed to amuse Lieutenant Kelly. I
thought his manner indicated, however, a little professional annoyance. An alibi, he seemed to say, de-
served more care than that.

"So you just sat there till midnight, you say.
Well, well."

He made a few scratches at his notebook, and put
it back in his pocket.

"Now, Mr. Wyndham, what was the last time
you was in your aunt's house?"

I thought there was perhaps the slightest hesitation.

"Three weeks ago," Chase said. He took a cigarette from the box on the table, and reaching in his pocket brought out a lighter. He lighted his cigarette and reached it over to Lieutenant Kelly, who had bit off the end of a stout cigar and was holding it poised. It was perfectly natural, of course, for Chase Wyndham to have a lighter—he's precisely the type of person who would—but it did seem to me, in view of what I'd told him, that he wouldn't flaunt it in the face of the detective. However, either Lieutenant Kelly hadn't heard about the mysterious signal from the window or was letting the matter pass.

"What'd you go for, Mr. Wyndham?" he said, blowing a large and apparently satisfying ring into the center of my living room.

"I had to see my aunt on business," Chase replied, flushing a little.

"Mind explaining?"

"No. I came down here chiefly because I persuaded my aunt a couple of years ago to insure her jewelry and the furniture and plate in the house against fire and theft. Also what the insurance people call 'mysterious disappearance.' "

He smiled mirthlessly.

"She did it, through a friend of mine in New York. She's had a number of losses in the last eight or ten months. Well, I met this fellow at a party a month or so ago, and he told me confidentially that his company was going to cancel the policy."

"What for?"

Chase shrugged.

"None of the stuff that disappeared has ever turned up. They sent a man down when the first two or three things went. It looked all right. But they've paid my aunt something like three thousand dollars. It isn't very much, of course, but the whole affair looked rather funny. I gathered from this fellow—he was tight, or he wouldn't have let all this out—that they weren't sure something serious mightn't happen. He didn't say just what. But the house is insured for $50,000 and the furniture for $30,000."

"Now the pearls are missing," remarked Lieutenant Kelly.

Chase grunted.

"Was that all you wanted to see the old lady for?"

"No, I wanted her to lend me ten thousand dollars. Which she did."

We both stared at him.

"She did?" said Lieutenant Kelly, who apparently had formed much the same opinion of Miss Nettie that everybody else had. He squinted at me again with his peculiar eyes.

"What sort of terms'd she give you?"

"Ten per cent," said Chase curtly. "For thirty days."

The wrinkles around Lieutenant Kelly's eyes deepened.

"Prepared to meet that note next week, Mr. Wyndham?" he inquired in a positively silky voice.

"No," said Chase quietly.

"I suppose you knew your aunt's will left you just exactly five dollars?"

"Yes. I knew it."

"Well, well," said Lieutenant Kelly. "Somebody's kindly stealing that will's a break for you, ain't it?"

He leaned forward with sardonic interest. A long gray cylinder of ash plopped unnoticed on my rug.

"Lieutenant," said Chase very easily, "that's the only break I've had since November, 1929."

CHAPTER

10

LIEUTENANT KELLY interviewed Eliot Wyndham and Gail before he left that morning. Eliot's story was precisely like his brother's. The two of them had dined with Gail, and left about nine o'clock. She was tired and wanted to go to bed. They didn't want to go back to the hotel, so decided to run out to Stonehill, where they'd lived as boys. They sat there talking until nearly midnight, and went back to their hotel.

Eliot knew nothing about his brother's previous visit to Miss Nettie, or about the ten thousand dollar loan at ten per cent for thirty days until that night at Stonehill, when Chase had told him about it.

"Worried about it, was he, Professor?"

"Naturally," Eliot said. "He knew she wouldn't hesitate to call it, and throw him into receivership. In fact, he'd quite made up his mind to it."

"Yeah?" said Lieutenant Kelly. "Well, that's interesting. Now, I understand the two of you just sat on the steps at this place you went to and smoked and talked?"

"That's right."

"He says you had a drink too?"

"We did."

"Where'd you get it?"

"My brother had a pint of rye in the car."

"How much'd you drink?"

"Not much. I had one drink. My brother probably two."

"He said I'd find the empty bottle under the
hedge," said Lieutenant Kelly dryly.

"Then I must have lost count."

"It would seem you'd killed the bottle."

"If we did I wasn't aware of it," said Eliot.

"But you only had one?"

He hesitated a little. Then he said, "That's right,
Lieutenant."

From Gail Lieutenant Kelly got nothing, or if
he did get anything I didn't notice it. She knew
nothing about Chase's visit to Miss Nettie, or about
his financial dealings with her. She had gone to bed
at nine o'clock. She'd had a hard day and was tired.
No, she wasn't fond of her aunt; in fact, she and
her aunt were bitter enemies. Everybody in town
knew it. Her aunt had treated her mother very
badly, had practically stolen the money Gail's
father left for them in her hands. Her father, as far
as she could make out, had been pretty well under
Miss Nettie's domination. He had taken his wife
to live there as soon as they were married. Miss
Nettie turned the two out the day he died.

Lieutenant Kelly listened with little interest. "When were you in the house last?" he said.

"Six years ago when my mother died. She sent for me and said I was to live with her. I was only fourteen then, but I was afraid. Dr. Fisher took me in."

"Of course you was there when they put up that tablet Tuesday," he reminded her. I thought he was impressed, as he might well be, by her dark, fragile beauty. He said later to me, "You don't often meet those kind in my job."

"I wasn't in the house," she said quickly. "I was on the porch. She wouldn't let me in. God knows I didn't want to go in."

"And you haven't been in since, I guess."

She shook her head.

Lieutenant Kelly left shortly afterwards. I thought—quite wrongly, as it turned out—that he was a little baffled by the three Wyndhams, who were so much alike and at the same time so different.

I telephoned just after he'd gone to see if I could get my hair washed, and was told that Miss Lake was busy for the rest of the afternoon. She'd been sent for by Mr. Taylor and a detective from Baltimore.

I could use my arm again, although it was still stiff and sore, and I was still a little annoyed at the way in which both Mr. Taylor and Lieutenant Kelly completely ignored it. I wondered if they thought my story was some elaborate and pointless

hoax. In any case, my vacation was over, and I
went my own afternoon rounds. Everyone was much
the same, a few of them three days better—which,
of course, they would have been, I'm afraid, whether
Dr. Wilkins or I or anybody else had called on them
or not. The new Thorntons were fine looking young
people, and old Miss Adams had died. However,
two for one was a fair ratio, and life is pretty much
like that.

I dropped in at the Pennimans' late in the afternoon, and found Alice, brisk and vigorous and
flighty again, deep in consultation with the asbestos
husband.

"You're just the person we want to see," she
said. "Samuel says he heard in town this morning
that Miss Wyndham's will has been destroyed."

Samuel looked at his wife sadly.

"No, Alice," he said gently. "I didn't say it was
destroyed. I said it had disappeared."

"It's the same thing. Somebody must have stolen
it, and if they stole it they certainly destroyed it
unless they're a complete fool. Well, anyway, Ruth,
is it true?"

"As far as I know it is," I replied. "I've been told
they've searched the house from cellar to garret for
it, too."

"Dear, dear," sighed Alice. "That means they'll
have to sell the house, of course."

Poor Alice! She couldn't disguise her utter satisfaction, and at the same time she certainly didn't want to seem to gloat.

"Not necessarily, dear," said Samuel.

"You said so!"

"No, dear. I said they'd have to divide the property between the four of them."

"It's the same thing. I'd like to see anybody divide a house into four without selling it. Unless, of course, they'd give Gail the house as her share. Why, that's an idea! I must tell Gail."

The asbestos man looked serious.

"Alice," he said soberly, "if I were you I'd keep out of this."

Samuel is a tired business man of the old school, sixty now, gouty, and retired except for monthly excursions to New York to look after various businesses.

"Nat'll go up next year," he always says, and Nat's mother always insists she can't get on without him at home another year.

"All right, just one more," Samuel agrees. He doesn't want him to go either. "You're making a molly-coddle out of the boy."

They both know, as a matter of fact, that instead they're making one of the best farmers in the country. Nat's making all their worn-out land pay more than it ever has.

"Well, of course, Samuel," Alice said, pouting as she always does when she doesn't get her way, "I think I ought to give the child advice. It's really my duty."

"If Gail needs advice," he replied, patting her arm gently, "I think Ruth had better do the giving. But from what I've seen of her I don't think she needs any advice, or would take it if you gave it to her."

"I just thought, Samuel, that if it's really Gail's share, then it would save your having to buy it at such an awful price. Wouldn't it be lovely for Gail and Nat to live there with us, Ruth?" she went on with a sudden return to her usual cheerfulness. "At last a Wyndham in the house to take care of it properly! I'm going to have Rittenhouse restore it. Won't it be marvelous!"

I glanced at Samuel. He was staring absently into the fire. I gathered of course that he'd been listening to this ever since the news of Miss Nettie's death got up the hill. As for Alice, she went on making her plans, and getting up and bringing me drawings of this and designs for that. Once, when she went into another room to bring me a sample of some material she'd sent for that day for the Wyndham house, I turned to her husband.

"I wouldn't encourage this, Samuel," I said. "If anything happens it will upset her terribly. Anything's likely to happen. This is all very uncertain. Don't you think?"

He nodded, rather grimly, I thought.

"Don't worry, Ruth," he said. "Nothing's going

to happen. Alice is going to get that house if it's the last thing I ever do."

Alice came back with a piece of deep cherry red bourette, just as Nat entered the room. His hands were thrust dejectedly into his pockets, his face terribly grave and unhappy.

We all stared at him.

"Why, what's the matter, Nat?"

He tossed his battered soft hat on the Phyfe sofa and sat down.

"It's Gail," he said. "She's given me the air."

Alice Penniman's eyes blazed like a tiger's whose cub has been attacked.

"That wretched, ungrateful girl!" she began. "I'll . . ."

Nat got up quickly.

"No, you won't, Mother," he said quietly, his jaw set. "That's what's wrong now. She says you're only willing to have me marry her because you think you'll get the house that way."

The asbestos man's face flushed angrily.

"Nat!" he said sternly. "I forbid you to speak to your mother that way!"

The two men stood for an instant glaring at one another. After a tense moment during which Alice stared in horror at both of them, Nat drew a sharp deep breath and relaxed.

"I'm sorry, Dad," he said. "Forgive me, Mother. Good-by, Doc." With that he went out of the room.

I left as quickly as I could, and drove down the

hill wondering if Gail was going to make a mess of things simply because her pride couldn't brook Alice Penniman's officiousness. Granting that at times it was most annoying, I still thought Gail would have sense enough to see that it was well meant, and to realize that really no kinder or more generous mortal than Alice existed.

I was thinking about that when I suddenly received a shock—to my egotism I suppose—which hurt me more than a really sensible person would have allowed it to do. I saw a large luxurious car with uniformed driver turn up the road, and recognized in the back Maxfield Burton, the Hopkins heart man. In spite of what I'd been thinking about Alice, I felt the sharpest twinge of professional jealousy. I'd known, of course, that they knew him, but I was sure they'd never sent for him before. Now, apparently, Samuel didn't think I was good enough to take care of his wife's heart. He was perfectly justified, of course, in calling in so distinguished a specialist if he chose, but I felt hurt that he hadn't told me he was going to do it.

I went home to dinner and sat down with the three young Wyndhams. They acted throughout the meal as if nothing unpleasant had happened since the Peasants' Revolt.

Gail and Eliot carried it off beautifully. Chase was a little drawn. His fine cut Wyndham features —high cheek-bones, thin sensitive nostrils, full sensuous mouth—seemed sharpened and pale. He

frequently smoothed his tiny black mustache with
his thumb and forefinger, and tugged at his collar
once or twice as if it was choking him. Still, he did
very well.

We left the table about eight o'clock. I went into
my office to see a colored friend of Estaphine's
whose husband had accidentally slashed her twice
with a razor. That over, I was getting ready to go
to the hospital, when the telephone rang.

It was Judge Garth's niece who was going to be
with him this winter. Her little boy had fallen in
the garden pool after lunch and had dried himself
without the formality of changing his clothes. He
had started to wheeze, and his mother wanted me to
stop by and have a look at him.

It was about half-past eight when I saw a curly-
headed, rosy-cheeked youngster who was perfectly
all right, or would be next morning, and reassured
his mother. I was just leaving when the colored man
came in and said Judge Garth would like to see me
before I left.

He was in his study, seated at an old walnut
desk. Mr. Taylor was on one side of the fireplace,
Lieutenant Kelly, perspiring unobtrusively, on the
other. A low blaze on the hearth made the room
terribly close, but Judge Garth looked chilly.

"You know these men, Dr. Fisher," he said, bowing. "Won't you sit down, please."

He indicated a chair which Mr. Taylor pushed
forward hastily.

"We were going to get in touch with you in the morning," Judge Garth continued deliberately, "as I want to give Mr. Taylor my evidence as a guest at Mrs. Penniman's and as a person summoned by Miss Wyndham. I have not yet quite decided if it is possible for me to try this case."

Mr. Taylor made a deprecatory gesture. I didn't quite understand.

"I see," I said. "Since I'm here can we do it now?"

"If you please. I would like you to check me if I have made any mistakes."

He took a piece of paper from his desk and read it slowly.

"Mrs. Penniman requested me to lunch with them Tuesday, after the unveiling of the tablet at Wyndham House. She said that Miss Wyndham would be present. I went out of respect to Mrs. Penniman and Miss Wyndham, who was an old and very close friend. Miss Wyndham was highly nervous, and insulted her niece and her hostess. She also threatened to burn the Wyndham house down, accused her hostess of trying to poison her, and in general acted in an unusual and offensive manner."

Lieutenant Kelly took out his two-inch stub of pencil. He used it by first moistening it and then bearing down very hard, and peering around under his fingers to see if it was writing.

"As a result of her tirade, Mrs. Penniman had an attack which Dr. Fisher has diagnosed as pseudo-

angina pectoris. She administered a tablet which
Nat Penniman got, at her request, from her bag on
the hall table. In his excitement he dropped the
pills. He picked them up after his mother was taken
upstairs.

"Miss Wyndham left, escorted by her nephew
Richard. The rest of us stayed. It was at this time
that Nat Penniman picked up the small phial con-
taining his mother's pills and said that some of them
were gone. People looked about but could not find
all of them.

"Eliot and Chase Wyndham left next. Gail
Wyndham and myself followed them, soon afterwards."

Lieutenant Kelly interrupted him.

"I guess it was possible for anybody in the room
to have picked up those pills, Judge?"

Judge Garth looked at me.

"Quite possible to have picked up some of them,
I should say," I replied.

"But I suppose you didn't see anybody do it?"

Judge Garth shook his head.

"I didn't," I said. "I was too busy with Mrs.
Penniman."

Judge Garth continued.

"I then came home. Shortly before four o'clock
that afternoon, Richard Wyndham telephoned me,
saying that his aunt wished to see me at once. When
I got there Dr. Fisher was already there. Miss
Wyndham said she wanted to give Miss Gail

Wyndham her pearls. She refused to have a codicil added to her will as I suggested. She requested me to get the will, which I did, and read the provisions leaving all of the property in her possession to her nephew Richard.

"She then requested Dr. Fisher to bring her jewel box from the bureau drawer and found at that time that the pearls were gone. Dr. Fisher went to call Richard Wyndham from downstairs, where he had taken Miss Wyndham's dog at her request. While she was gone Miss Wyndham went back to her bed. I went to the bathroom and brought her a glass of fresh water. She drank a little of it and put it on the table by her bed. I left the house after Dr. Fisher came back with Richard, who had telephoned to the police."

Judge Garth put the paper down on his desk.

"That, gentlemen," he said, "is to the best of my memory the exact order of events preceding Antoinette Wyndham's death. It is necessary for you to find out who introduced poison into that glass of water, between the time it came from the tap, around four o'clock that afternoon, and the time Miss Wyndham drank it, before she went to bed for the night. It will also be necessary for you to find out who removed her will from the house after I had read it, and before the theft of the pearls was discovered. That, gentlemen, is your task."

He rose and bowed, and in an amazingly short

space of time the three of us found ourselves out on the porch, the judicial door closed behind us.

"Good night, Mr. Taylor," I said. "Good night, Lieutenant Kelly."

"Good night, Doctor."

Then Lieutenant Kelly came back to my car and said, "Oh, by the way, Doctor. Would you mind coming around to that place"——he nodded towards Wyndham House——"and show me just about where you got that crack on the arm?"

"I'd be glad to," I said.

That night I had a call about half-past eleven that took me across the bridge and out the mountain road. It was after one o'clock when I came back through the deserted Court House Square. The scarlet-and-gold-leafed maples made gorgeous shades for the street lights, and the empty streets impressed me, as they always do late at night, with the unreality of all the bustle and confusion of the day.

For some reason I can't determine, unless it's that I'm just a natural-born busybody, I didn't turn my car into Gloucester Road, which would have brought me to my own door. I kept on down Chase Street, and turned right, into Charles Street in front of Wyndham House. It couldn't have been a premonition, for the simple reason that I don't believe in premonitions. But it was something, call it a restless curiosity, that made me stop at the front gate and peer in through the iron bars, past the two giant black magnolias, up the garden walk. At first I thought the light of the waning moon was playing optical tricks on me. Then I got out of my car and tip-toed to the gate. It was open a few inches.

Still hardly aware of what, if anything, I expected to find in that garden, I pushed the gate open far enough to get through, and closed it after me.

Seen from between those grand magnolias, Wyndham House, lying beautifully symmetrical and perfect at the end of the garden walk, seemed curiously vital and alive. It didn't have the closed, deserted air of most old, shuttered houses in which life appears to have stopped—even if some old person still occupies them. With Miss Nettie gone, it seemed as if some fearful nimbus had lifted from the high brick chimneys rising from the roof, and the house was at last at peace with itself and the lovely gardens that surrounded it.

I was thinking that when I saw a sudden flash of light in the elaborate fan light over the door appear and disappear, appear again and vanish. I knew at once that it was a flashlight, and that obviously someone was carrying it through the dark rooms of Wyndham House. Who was it? What was he hunting? Those questions burned in my mind, and I thought of the will and the jewels.

Then the light appeared again, for the fraction of an instant, in the Palladian window over the door. Which way it was going I couldn't tell; the other windows were tightly shuttered. But I knew that upstairs was the room in which old Miss Nettie had died, and that it was the room in which she had kept—and lost—her will and her jewels.

Without particularly thinking what it might mean, I went quickly across the grass and around the house to the right. Almost unconsciously I figured that anyone entering there would do so from the rear. I tried the hyphen door; it opened. I stepped inside. I was in the passage between the house and the wing where I had come upon Richard Wyndham staring down at the heel-marks on the cellar landing. I closed the door and stood, breathless, listening to the faint noises in the old house, trying to distinguish what was human from what was old house and rodent. Suddenly, quite close to me and above my head, I heard a creak, and another. I knew very well, from my experience the night of Miss Nettie's death, what that meant. Someone was coming stealthily down the stairway.

I took my small flashlight out of my coat pocket and pressed the switch. In an instant of light I saw that the door into the main house was closed, and that half the cellar door was open. As quickly and silently as I could I made for the cellar opening, turned the flashlight into it, and went cautiously down the steps.

I remembered it only dimly from the night Daphne Lake and I were there.

Then I heard the door upstairs open, and saw the faint glow from the light in the hyphen.

I stood barely daring to trust the sound of my own breathing, waiting. Would whoever it was go out, or would they come down? Slowly I felt my way in the pitch dark to a door that I'd noticed set in the thick foundation stone. I figured that it must correspond roughly with the breakfast room upstairs. Chancing it, I stepped over its threshold and pressed the switch of my light. It was a room filled with old milk pails and jars, covered with countless spider webs and layers of dust.

Inside I waited. Then I saw a circle of light on the cellar floor. Through the tiny crack of the nearly closed door I watched it flatten out and become larger as the hand that carried it came slowly and very quietly down the steps.

For the next five minutes, I suppose, which seemed like as many months, I watched that light play hide and seek around the great stone pillars. In and out it went, resting, it seemed, on each stone and each brick. Still I couldn't see who carried it. I knew it was a man, because once the beam caught his foot. I saw a brown pebbled leather shoe and the gray cuff of a tweed trouser leg. I didn't recognize them.

I can't say how long this had gone on when suddenly I heard a sharp click upstairs. My unknown friend heard it too. The light behind the stone pillar supporting the great chimneys went out hastily, and I heard a hurried movement. Then everything was silent, except for the swift light movements upstairs. Then another light flashed down the steps, and another pair of almost noiseless feet came down, this time quickly and unhesitatingly. There were three of us in the cellar of Wyndham House.

The light was lower this time. For a moment my heart nearly stopped, the blood chilled in my veins. Then suddenly it flashed up. I saw in the middle of the heavy shadows of the blackness the wide brown eyes and white-gold hair of Daphne Lake.

I knew the man in the corner must have seen her too. She was unconscious of anyone else there. Quickly and unerringly she went to the center shaft of stone that is arched to support the great weight above, and bending down, stepped into the arch. She turned her light up and down the masonry, and then stooped down.

She propped the flashlight on the ground against a brick so that it lighted the face of the masonry, and with both hands removed a long thin strip of mortar, and laid it carefully beside her light. Then she tugged with both hands until the rough stone, on the surface perhaps a foot square, came out. She eased it down to the floor, picked up her light and turned its beam into the cavity.

She was breathing quickly. Holding the light then in her left hand, she put her right hand into the hole, and suddenly drew out a glittering object. I recognized it at once—it was the famous Wyndham coffee pot. Suddenly, like a lovely wild animal, she swiftly replaced it, and threw back her head and listened. A round shaft of light came from the other side of the cellar, focusing its yellow beam on the kneeling girl.

A voice out of the darkness said, with quiet mockery, "So that's the game, is it, Daphne Lake?"

II

DAPHNE LAKE rose slowly to her feet, and brought her light up until its beam outlined the dark face of Richard Wyndham, smiling bitterly at her.

"Hairdresser or thief?" he said quietly. The cruel scorn in his voice cut like a whip.

She stiffened, and her breath came in quick audible starts. But she was silent.

Richard Wyndham took a step forward so that he was standing close to her, his light full in her face. His face was dark with contempt and anger. With a sudden movement he seized her wrist. Her light flew out of her hand, leaving the man only a cool derisive voice in the dark.

"Where's my aunt's will?" he said suddenly.

I saw her lithe body start with the pain of his pressure on her hand. Still she said nothing.

"Who paid you to steal it?" he said savagely, between his closed teeth.

"Nobody!" she said coolly.

"You're lying. You've been lying to me for six months. It's over now. Get over there!"

She moved suddenly a little to one side, and then,

before I could see what had happened, I heard her voice, tense and icy.

"Give me that light, and keep your hands up!"

I saw her take the light out of his hand, and I saw the glint of blue steel. Daphne Lake was pressing an automatic revolver against his body.

"Turn around," she said sharply. "Go up those stairs and get out of this house. If you were found in here, you'd be in worse trouble than you are now."

I heard him swear softly under his breath.

In five minutes I was alone in the cellar. Fifteen minutes later I was at home. I knew that both Daphne and Richard must have seen my car parked in front of the gate, on their way out. I went to sleep wondering what they'd do about it.

When I drove up to Wyndham House seven hours later, Lieutenant Kelly was waiting for me. He got down to business at once.

"All right, now," he said. "You was here around midnight, Wednesday, and half-past three or so in the afternoon. I want you to just come around with me and tell me what you did both times. I want you to tell me anything you saw that looks like it had any connection here."

I didn't reply directly to that, as there were several things, one of them the scene in the cellar the night before, that I had no intention of telling him.

"Richard Wyndham let me in the front door," I

said, "and showed me into the small drawing-room here."

We were standing in the hall. I pointed to the door on the left.

"He told me he thought the day had been too much for his aunt. Otherwise he didn't make any apology for the way she acted. After a minute or two we went upstairs to see Miss Wyndham."

He nodded, and we started up. As we went I realized how different the house was, now that the shutters were open. The autumn light came in on the gorgeous carved mantels and doors, showing the perfect rooms filled with lovely things, still carefully kept. There was nothing broken down or unkempt in Wyndham House or in the garden.

Lieutenant Kelly unlocked Miss Nettie's bedroom door and held it open while I entered. Everything was the same, except that Miss Nettie and her dog were gone, and the tumbler that held the fatal drink of water.

He looked at me inquiringly.

"I came in and sat down here," I said, pointing to the side of the bed. "Miss Wyndham was lying here. She said she wasn't ill. She wanted to make a gift of her pearls to her niece, Gail Wyndham, who lives with me. She'd sent her nephew Richard to phone to Judge Garth, who came over at once. While the three of us were talking she sent her nephew out with her dog. It was then that she asked

Judge Garth to get her will and read it; and then that she discovered the pearls were missing.

"I went downstairs and got her nephew. He was standing in the hyphen—that's the passage between the house and the wing. He was looking down the cellar steps. . . ."

"Hey, wait a minute, Doctor," he said. "Tell me about that when we get down there. Now about them pearls. When you were here, the old lady and the judge in the room, the boy downstairs somewhere, you went over to the drawer there to get the pearls. That right?"

"Yes. I brought the velvet case over to the table here. She was lying on the bed in her street clothes. She got up and came to this table to get the pearls. I saw her open the box."

"So when we found your finger-prints on that drawer, that's how they came to be there."

I was naturally startled. The idea of taking my finger-prints hadn't occurred to me. The mesh of fine lines deepened around Lieutenant Kelly's eyes.

"We've got everybody's prints," he said complacently. "Now, then. When young Wyndham comes up, what does he do?"

"Young Wyndham," I said, "spoke to his aunt. He said he didn't think it was much use to call the police, but he went and did it anyway."

"You didn't stay after that?"

"No."

"Judge Garth put the will back in the desk there.

I guess you didn't ever see the old lady or the nephew get it again."

I looked at him in surprise.

"Why, no. There'd be no point in Richard's taking the will—he was the sole legatee."

Lieutenant Kelly looked at me as much as to say that there was a lot I didn't know about things.

"The old lady could have destroyed that will herself," he said, with a queer look at me. "If she was going to give the niece something, she might have made up her mind to change the whole darn thing. And don't forget this, Doctor, if the old lady had half an idea of burning the house up, and I was her nephew, and she'd left everything to me in a will, you can bet I'd get that will out of the house first thing I could."

"In that case," I said, "Richard would bring it forward."

"Not right now," said Lieutenant Kelly sardonically. "Not so you'd notice it. Not when somebody's murdered the old lady. Though it's pretty obvious if he stole the will he didn't do in the old lady, and if he did do her in, then some other guy hooked the will."

"That sounds reasonable," I said.

He changed the subject abruptly from Richard to his aunt.

"Michaels says she'd been dead about four hours when he saw her."

"Or five, or six," I said. "You can't tell that closely, in a person of her age."

"Well, then," he said. "That's got her dying somewhere around nine o'clock. All right. That gets us to this. This Richard says he left here about ten minutes after Miss Lake came. Miss Lake says the old woman was alive when she said good night to her and closed her door. That was half-past eight."

I waited, not seeing at the moment what he was getting at.

"All right. Now then. This Richard is afraid the old woman's going to burn the house down. He and this platinum blonde down at the beauty shop are pretty thick. That's right, ain't it?" he demanded abruptly.

"I understand they go around together quite a bit."

"Yeah. Well then, his word ain't worth a tinker's damn, nor hers neither."

One of the nice things about Lieutenant Kelly was his perfect confidence that he knew exactly what he was talking about. In view of that, I refrained from casting any doubt on the theory he was advancing as we stood there, looking around old Miss Nettie's room.

It was queer to be there. The whole atmosphere was heavy with drugs and death. The battery of medicine bottles with stained labels, and the package of prepared dog food behind them on the table, made the air unpleasantly like the back room of

Miggs's Negro drug store on Constitution Street. The dress Miss Nettie wore that afternoon was lying across the back of a lovely painted Sheraton chair. It had been dragged on the floor; the shoulders were covered with dusty dirt. It had that unclean odor that clothes belonging to the dead always seem to me to have, no matter how clean they really are.

I don't know much about the business of detection, which seemed to give Lieutenant Kelly a good deal of quiet enjoyment. He explained to me how they take finger-prints. He pointed out three or four sets that still showed under the whitish-gray powder they had been dusted with.

"Those there," he said, pointing with the end of a yellow pencil, "are yours."

He chuckled.

"Don't suppose you'd figured out I got them last night from the prescription you left the kid at the judge's."

"No, I didn't," I admitted as casually as I could. I began to feel that Lieutenant Kelly was subtler than the new dove gray felt hat indicated.

"Well, I did. And they match this lot here. In fact, Doctor, they're all over the house. Downstairs on the living room table. I guess that's what you call it—that long room where the big lamp is."

I nodded.

"And plenty of them in the cellar."

"Cellar?" I said.

"Yes, ma'am. The cellar. That surprise you?"

"No, it doesn't," I said, quite honestly.

"Well, now," he rejoined, "it did me."

He bit off the end of one of his appalling cigars.

"Because," he went on, "there's a lot of them there this morning that wasn't there yesterday when we took the pictures. So I had to have 'em take a lot more. They're down there now."

"How do you know they weren't there yesterday?" I asked, with as much coolness as I could muster.

He grinned.

"Because, Doctor, when I look at things I make it a point to see them. That's part of my business. Well, now, this morning there's a lot of things down there that I'd of seen if they'd of been there to see. The camera'll prove if I'm right, but I don't lose any sleep about that."

"Are you always right, Lieutenant?" I asked, without any desire at all to be sardonic.

He seemed to understand perfectly.

"I'm always right about details like that, that concern my own job," he said. "The times I'm wrong are when I've got to decide about things that ain't so definite as finger-prints on a dusty wall, or a long yellow hair caught on a beam."

"I see," I said.

He laid his cigar precariously on the edge of a mahogany dresser that was worth Alice Penniman's right arm—the price she usually sets on such things

—and completely ignored the damning fact of Daphne's hair as if it weren't worth mentioning.

"Well, now," he said. "Here's your prints, and here's the old lady's. Yours are on top of hers. She opened the drawer before you did. But we can't find anybody else's there."

He took another puff at his cigar and laid it down again.

"Here's Judge Garth's prints over here," he went on, going to the secretary and pointing with his pencil at the imprint in the powder on the closed slant top of the desk.

"And here's somebody else's on top of his, and here's somebody else's on top of parts of both of 'em. I got to admit I'm sure getting a break here. People's don't leave their prints lying about all over the lot the way they used to."

"Does that mean that two people beside Judge Garth opened this desk after he did?"

"That's what it means."

"Do you know who they are?"

"I sure do, Dr. Fisher," replied Lieutenant Kelly. "And I'm going to show you something else. And then I'm going to show you something else beside that. And then I'm going to ask you to play the game with me, straight and aboveboard. You know, Doctor, I don't want to arrest that girl. I got a girl of my own just about her age. I don't like to be hard on 'em. Now look here."

I followed his pencil around the room.

Every drawer handle had been dusted, and every one showed a small finely ridged imprint.

"A woman left those marks, Doctor," he said. "They're on everything in the house. You see most of this stuff wasn't touched very much, and I guess the nigger didn't dust every day, nor anywheres near it. I figure some of these here were made some days ago. Well, now. Downstairs they're on every blessed thing. Door knobs, picture frames, china vases, silver bowls. Now I want you to just climb up here and have a look."

He pushed a chair forward and held the back of it while I got up on it and looked at the top of the wide shelf made by the door frame. Along the edge, in the fine film of dust, were eight finger marks where someone had held on while she raised herself to look.

"See how they're flattened?" Lieutenant Kelly directed. "She's in a hurry. Didn't want to fetch a chair over. Just caught hold and pulled herself up. Strong girl."

I got down, feeling a distinct feeling of uneasiness about all this.

"Now then, Doctor. The question is, what's she looking for?"

He looked at me blandly.

"And the answer is, she's looking for the old lady's jewels."

I felt it was reasonable enough, in view of his evidence, and in view of my own observations I couldn't have much doubt of it, no matter how much I'd have liked to believe something else. Indeed, I could have told him where they were. But his confidence in himself was so infectious that I hadn't any doubt he would find out for himself very shortly, if he hadn't already done so.

"We'll go down cellar now, ma'am, if you please," he said, opening the door. He locked it carefully and we started down.

"Just a minute, first, though. I'll take a look in here."

We went into the room Daphne had occupied that night and glanced around. Her things were all there except the cigarette lighter. I missed it at once. Apparently Lieutenant Kelly merely wanted to look at the room. He didn't say anything until we were going downstairs. Then he remarked indifferently that it would be hard for some girls to stay four hours in a house with a dead woman, but that yellow-headed frail at the beauty shop had the nerve of a brass monkey so he didn't suppose she'd mind.

Recalling the terror in Daphne Lake's voice over the telephone at midnight that Wednesday, I thought he was wrong. Recalling the sight of her slim body swaying under Richard Wyndham's grip in the cellar the night before, and her cool metal-edged order as she stuck her revolver into his stomach, I wasn't so sure.

We came down stairs. I remembered the night

when Daphne confronted Richard in the hall before she fled out into the night. I thought then that she was in love with him. I was certain he was in love with her. I wondered now what had happened. All I could think of very clearly was his accusation thrown at her with all the bitterness and anger in his soul: "Who paid you to steal the will?"

Dear, dear, I thought, and pulled myself together to listen to Lieutenant Kelly. "What strikes me," he was saying, "is she didn't miss a trick in the house. Now, why didn't she wear gloves? That's the question, and I'll bet if I could give you the answer I'd know something, and don't you forget it, Doctor. The only answer I can give you now is, she didn't know the old dame was done in. Either that or she never thought there'd be any question about it."

Again I remembered Daphne Lake's asking me why I couldn't give the death certificate without calling in Dr. Michaels.

Lieutenant Kelly pointed to the cellar doors exactly as if he thought I'd never seen them before.

"Well, well," he said. "I guess this is the cellar." I caught some quiet enjoyment in his voice.

He opened both sides of the door.

"I'll go first," he said, turning a powerful lamp onto the dim half-daylight below.

The place looked different, somehow, and less awful. I overcame my impulse to look behind each pillar as we passed it.

"I'd like you to look here first, Doctor," he said,

and led me straight to the very spot I'd occupied during the scene between Daphne and Richard Wyndham eight hours before.

"Here you are, now."

He pointed to the floor.

"Those are your shoes. Not the ones you got on now, but a pair of brown sneakers. I got them from your maid this morning when you was at the hospital."

"Oh," I said.

"And this here is where you leaned against the wall."

He brought the beam up and showed me my perfectly imprinted hand on the dusty surface of the whitewashed stones.

"Now then. I guessed you must of been watching something pretty good. So I looked straight over there first thing. This is what I found."

He strode across the packed earth floor and knelt down, almost in the exact spot Daphne had knelt in. He pulled out the long strip of mortar and let down the stone. I looked past him into the hole.

"It was empty when I opened it this morning," he said, looking up at me. "Where are the pearls, Doctor?"

"I don't know, I'm sure," I said. It was an entirely truthful answer.

"What's your guess, then?"

He eyed me with a sort of determined patience.

"Lieutenant Kelly," I said, "I haven't got one."

CHAPTER

12

LOOKING back on that morning, I find that my chief trouble was that I persisted in underestimating Lieutenant Kelly. However, I at least no longer took him at his own simple rating of a detective who knew his job.

He turned away from the empty hole at the bottom of the arch and brushed off his knees.

"Now let's see," he said, apparently dismissing the pearls. "When you came downstairs Wednesday afternoon to get young Wyndham, where'd you say he was?"

"Up there in the hyphen. He was looking down here."

"I guess the door flaps was laid back?"

"One of them certainly was. I don't remember that both were."

"And you thought somebody was down here?"

"Yes," I said. "He'd said something about hearing someone when he went upstairs first."

"You hear anybody?"

"I heard what he heard, but I thought it was a rat."

152

Lieutenant Kelly nodded and got out another cigar.

"When I came downstairs," I went on, "after Miss Wyndham found the pearls gone, he was looking down here. I told him what had happened. He let down the cellar doors and fastened the padlock in the hasp. He said something about my being right about the burglar. I thought he was lying. I had the impression that he did think somebody was down here, and that he knew who it was."

"I guess you thought he was shielding somebody."

"Exactly."

"You didn't come down here again?"

"Not until that night Miss Lake phoned for me. She and I came down together."

"Cellar doors open then?"

"Yes."

"So young Wyndham must of unlocked them before he went home."

"I guess so."

"All right, Doctor," he said. "Now look at this."

We crossed the passage and went through another door on the same side of the cellar as the room that I'd been in. We stopped to get through the low deep doorway, and found ourselves in a room with beams set with hooks.

"This is where they used to hang the meat, I guess," Lieutenant Kelly said, and continued across the room until we came under the narrow window set in the thick stone wall. This window was perhaps a little over a foot high and three feet from side to side, and gave out into a narrow bricked well, now filled with brown leaves from the tulip poplars in the back garden. It was probably six feet from the cellar floor.

He pointed with his cigar at the new scratches on the whitewashed walls, and at the loose bolts on the bottom of the window frame.

"Somebody climbed up here and went through this window," he said rather obviously.

I agreed.

He assumed an air of profound mystery.

"You see what it means?"

"Yes," I said. "It means that whoever was here got out before Richard Wyndham got back—or the police, if they looked around."

"Sure," he said. He seemed rather proud of me for being that bright. "And it means whoever it was was small enough to get through that hole. And that means it most likely was a woman."

I nodded.

"Well, then. Wyndham was shielding a woman. We got to assume it was this Miss Lake. You know anything about her?"

"I know she came to town six months ago, got a job in the beauty parlor, and seems a very capable and efficient young woman," I said.

"She runs around with this fellow?"

"Constantly."

He wagged his head.

"Then you think it was this Miss Lake was down here, and not Gail Wyndham?"

"I hadn't thought of its being Gail," I said a little indignantly. "I couldn't think of her doing such a thing."

"You couldn't?" said Lieutenant Kelly.

There was good-natured tolerance in his tone.

"Then you just come with me."

Together we made our way back into the main passage of the cellar and up the steps into the hyphen. Then he apparently changed his mind.

"You said you climbed over the wall when you came here that night."

He tried not to look incredulous. I'll admit the idea of my climbing about over walls isn't as credible as it might have been twenty years ago.

"Believe it or not," I said, and we both laughed.

"Why didn't you come in the gate?"

"The gate's always locked, so I assumed it was that night. I thought Miss Lake wouldn't have the keys to unlock it. Old John always carries them. I didn't think she'd want to go wandering about looking for them."

"Well, *were* they locked?"

"I don't know. Miss Lake got John out to let in the coroner when we sent for him."

He grunted.

"That girl tells me she went to your place just

before seven to tell you she was coming here. What'd she do that for?"

"She wanted somebody to know she was here."

"Well, well," he said. It seemed his favorite sardonic expression. "Richard Wyndham knew she was here. And somebody else knew it. Besides you."

"Really?" I said. "Who?"

"I ain't quite sure."

Lieutenant Kelly aimed his cigar at the large yellow head of a chrysanthemum, and flicked the ash with a neat movement of his diamond-ringed little finger. The gray flaky cylinder fell with perfect accuracy into the heart of the flower.

"But you remember," he went on, "when she signaled the car at the corner from the upper window."

I took that standing. Of course it was the first intimation I'd had that Lieutenant Kelly knew about my second visit to Charles Street.

"Young Abbott told Taylor about it yesterday. Said you'd advised him to."

I smiled.

"I did—in a sense."

"But you didn't think he'd do it?"

"I wasn't sure he would."

"Well, he did."

"And you've spoken to Miss Lake about it?"

"No," said Lieutenant Kelly easily. "I gave her a chance to tell me. But she didn't. I thought we'd let it ride a day or two."

We had been walking down the garden path towards Front Street during this conversation. We stopped at one point, and Lieutenant Kelly indicated a place on the wall where the vines had been badly torn and the earth below looked as if a ton of brick had landed on it.

"I guess that's where you came over," he said soberly, without as much as a crinkle around his eyes.

I guessed it was too.

"'S a wonder you didn't break your ankle," he said, shaking his head. "Now, sometime you might want to jump down from a wall again. So I'm just going to show you how to do it."

I had the natural feeling that he was getting some amusement out of this, but there was no sign of it in his manner.

"It's a matter of *technique*," he added. He reached up to the top of the wall, grasped it firmly, and swung himself up in one easy movement, with the agility of a monkey. He looked down at me from the top with an air of modest satisfaction.

I really stared at him open-mouthed, which seemed to please him.

"You tore your coat," he remarked, holding up a couple of gray tweed threads. "In case you don't know it. I noticed that this morning when the maid showed it to me. Now then. See how I come down."

He put one hand on the wall, balanced himself, and swung easily and lightly down to the ground.

"You see? You couldn't tell whether the fellow that landed there weighed more than a hundred pounds or not," he said simply. "It's just knowing how."

"Thank you," I said. "If I ever have to do it again, I'll try to remember. What did you think when you saw my tracks? Or did Mr. Taylor tell you about it?"

He let his voice fall confidentially.

"Mr. Taylor didn't tell me anything," he said. "No lawyer's going to put me off the track by telling me things. I look for myself. He can tell me what he wants me to think afterwards. See?"

He put the tweed threads from my coat in his pocket.

"Just in case you forget you climbed over there," he remarked with a wink. "Now then. Let's go over here and see what you think about this."

He cut across the grass to the wall that runs along the back of the Wyndham place. There's a narrow street there, Fleet Street it's called, whether after Fleet Street in London or because a fleet once anchored in the river and could be approached from there I don't know. I imagine that when the town was growing up, long before the Revolution, men were homesick for familiar names and places, and these names recalled home and England. At any rate, we have a Threadneedle Street, a Paternoster Row, and Holborn Hill that's since been changed to Madison Place.

Fleet Street isn't much. It's mostly littered up with boxes from the three rival chain grocery stores that face on Taney Street. It's just wide enough for a truck and a Negro to pass if the Negro squeezes up against Miss Nettie's wall and the trucks run against the fence on the other side. When it rains Fleet Street becomes a minor river.

"Watch your step there," warned Lieutenant Kelly as we came towards the wall. "I want you to have a look here."

He pointed to a trampled bed of autumn crocuses at the bottom of the wall under the big maple in the corner. I looked, and saw that somebody else who didn't know much about the technique of wall jumping had been there.

"Now then," he said, "look here."

He knelt down and pointed with his cigar. I saw a perfect footprint, and then another, in the clayish soil.

"They lifted the woman down," Lieutenant Kelly remarked casually. "She didn't touch the ground until she got over here."

Again he pointed with his cigar, this time to the edge of the bed where the grass was growing in thin uneven patches. I saw a woman's footprint, high-heeled, narrow-soled. At the edge I noticed a couple of white lumps.

"That's plaster of Paris," he said. "I took the impressions yesterday. I've been expecting somebody to do something about these things."

He indicated the footprints with a certain fastidious distaste. "So I left the plaster there just to make it a sporting proposition."

I looked at him, not understanding. He grinned.

"Well, you see, if they tried to mess up those footprints, it wouldn't be so good for them. Show they was afraid. And I've already got the impressions, see? So, if they wanted to take a chance on me not having spotted them, I thought it was fair to leave a piece of the cast, in case they had sense enough to see it."

"Is that what you call sporting?" I asked.

He gave me another sardonic wink.

"I got to admit the deck's stacked," he said. "Because I already know who they belong to."

Then I saw something that I guessed Lieutenant Kelly hadn't seen; and nothing could have given me a more sinking feeling in the pit of my stomach. Under a leaf just in the fringe where the grass wasn't clipped, I saw a small white pellet. I knew instantly, as certainly as if I held the formula for it in my hand, what that pill was made of and where it had come from.

Lieutenant Kelly was interested in the wall, his back turned to me. I had a sudden impulse to pick up that tiny damning hundredth-grain of digitalin and crumble it in my pocket. I knew I had no right to do it. I didn't even know whose high heels had made the deep hollow in the soft earth there. There was no reason at all for me to destroy evidence that had to lead, eventually, to Miss Nettie's murderer paying the supreme penalty. In fact, it was foolish to do it.

All that flashed through my mind, and I glanced at Lieutenant Kelly's broad back and stooped down swiftly and picked up the pellet.

"I'd leave that be, if I was you," he said seriously, without bothering to turn around. "I left it there apurpose. Got another just like it in my pocket."

I put the pill down in the exact spot where I'd got it, and felt myself flushing uncomfortably.

As I was very much annoyed I said, probably unpleasantly, "I suppose that was another of your sporting propositions, Lieutenant Kelly."

He had turned around now.

"No," he said imperturbably, shoving that gray hat back onto his cerebellum and scratching his crisp iron-gray hair. "I call that a trap."

"For me to fall into."

"That's the trouble with traps," he said, replacing his hat in its proper tilted angle over his forehead. "You got to take what you get—fisherman's luck."

"I see," I said.

"Well, now," he said, "that's what I wanted to show you."

He had exactly the air of quiet professional satisfaction that Samuel Penniman has when he looks up from the morning paper and says, "Well, I see asbestos is up a point."

Lieutenant Kelly and I sat down on a garden bench and silently regarded the rear elevation of Wyndham House. I'm not sure what he was thinking about. From the expression on his face, and the fat, billowy rings of pungent smoke he propelled in leisurely succession from his mouth, it might have been anything of a perfectly satisfactory nature.

For myself, I was trying to make sense out of the jumble of clues that he'd handed me. That Gail was involved in some way in this terrible thing was now impossible to try to disregard. Lieutenant Kelly knew that he didn't have to tell me that the girl "they" lifted over the wall was Gail Wyndham. It was pretty plain also that "they" were Chase and Eliot.

Yet I couldn't imagine Gail in this thing. After all, twenty-year-old girls don't go around giving poison to their aunts. While I was reassuring myself of that, I was uneasily aware that they've been known to do much worse things. I'm afraid that I really couldn't regard Miss Nettie's death as anything but a swift stroke of avenging justice. Heaven knows she'd been nothing more than a rapacious old vulture gnawing at the very life of the town and the people in it for fifty years. The list of the injustices that the old woman had inflicted was as long as the years that she'd lived, solitary and merciless, behind the brick walls in front of me.

"Did they ever show you the cartoon they had in the local paper one Christmas about this old woman, Lieutenant Kelly?" I asked suddenly, turning to him.

"No. What was it?"

"It was a picture of a spider behind four walls in the center of a web. The threads of the web ran through the walls. At the end of each was some pitiful example of what she'd done. The woman she'd evicted kneeling by a little grave—the baby died of pneumonia—; a church with the doors and windows nailed up because they couldn't pay their mortgage. All sorts of things like that."

He grinned tolerantly.

"What happened to the editor?"

"He left town. Miss Wyndham bought the paper. We didn't have any for a year."

"No great loss?"

"No."

"Well," he said, "you can't just go around poisoning people, now, can you?"

I agreed.

"And you got to admit this, Doctor. The people that got that will was thinking about Number One. Not about evicted babies."

"That's quite right," I admitted. "I'm not defending anybody, really. I just think it's too bad there isn't a better way of managing such things."

"You'd get into lots of trouble if you tried it," said Lieutenant Kelly.

Social philosophy wasn't his line—or mine either, for that matter. And I did have to admit that he'd hit the nail on the head when he said that the people who'd stolen Miss Nettie's will had no high ideal of social justice in front of them.

"The motive matters a whole lot, you know, Doctor," he said with a kind of gruff kindliness in his voice. "I don't care about the old so-and-so being bumped off. But I think it's a lousy trick to do it to get her jack."

"I guess so," I said. "That's right."

"Sure it's right. Well, now. You got to be careful about how much of this you let out."

He waved his hand over towards the footprints near the wall.

Then I did a rather odd thing. I was as surprised as Lieutenant Kelly when I turned towards him abruptly and said, "Do you know who writes these poison-pen letters?"

"What poison-pen letters?" he said after a little pause.

"The ones Gail receives," I replied.

"No, I don't," he said. "But I'm looking for the typewriter that wrote this."

He produced a bulky bill-fold and took out a folded slip of cheap letter paper. He handed it over to me. I unfolded it.

"That's it," I said.

He nodded and put it back in the bill-fold.

"That's supposed to be from Gail to her aunt," he said, looking queerly at me. "The only finger-prints I could find on it are old Miss Wyndham's and Daphne Lake's."

CHAPTER

13

W HEN I came home to lunch I was surprised to find Gail curled up in the corner of the sofa in the living room reading a magazine. Her job as Alice Penniman's social secretary normally keeps her away until the late afternoon. I hadn't taken her falling out with Nat as seriously, I suppose, as I should have done.

"I've quit being Mrs. Penniman's functotum," she announced with amiable malice. "In fact I'm carrying on the Wyndham tradition. I'm never going to put my foot in her house again."

I sat down and took off my hat.

"That's too bad," I said. "Did you just decide that, or have you got a reason?"

"I've got a dozen reasons," she replied promptly. She reached for a cigarette and lighted it with deadly calmness.

"One of them being that you don't need fifty dollars a month any longer?" I said, and was instantly sorry that I had. Quick tears sprang into her eyes.

"*Please*, Aunt Ruth!" she said. "You don't really think that, do you?"

"No, of course not," I said. "Alice undoubtedly does."

"I know she does. She gave me a frightful going over this morning. She said I'd been willing enough to marry Nat as long as I was penniless. I pointed out to her that the opposite was true as far as she was concerned. And anyway that it was my business and not hers."

"I hope this wasn't as bad as it sounds," I said. "Worse."

She tossed her cigarette into the fireplace.

"It was much worse. She started to weep. I was scared stiff she'd have an attack. So I put her pills and stuff on the table and ran away."

"Did you see Mr. Penniman before you left?"

"He was out somewhere."

She got up and moved slowly over to the window, and stood looking out into the garden.

"Aunt Ruth," she said after a moment, without turning around, "will you tell me what you think about all this?"

I didn't answer because I heard Estaphine's uneven tread in the hall.

"Lunch is served, Doctuh," she said with well-trained formality, and added severely, "An' yo' ain' got yo' hains washed yet! We don' wan' no hospital germs aroun' heah."

I sat at my end of the luncheon table looking at

Gail Wyndham across a centerpiece of tawny garden chrysanthemums.

"You didn't answer me," she said when Estaphine had gone back to the kitchen.

"I don't know what I think, Gail," I said, wondering what Lieutenant Kelly would say if his daughter with blue-black hair and deep appealing velvety eyes asked him that question. "What do you think about it?"

"I don't know either," she said, and was silent for a moment.

"Aunt Ruth," she said then suddenly, looking across at me with a troubled little line between her glossy arched brows, "do you think you can tell when people are telling the truth?"

"Not always," I said readily. "It depends on a great many, many things, usually."

"I know. But I mean somebody you . . . sort of know how they feel . . . because it's sort of the way you feel too. That's not very clear, is it? But that's what I mean."

"You can feel an absolute emotional conviction about what someone says," I admitted, not being sure about the value of such a conviction but knowing that I myself had them a good deal.

"That's what I thought," she said calmly.

I hadn't of course the faintest notion of what she was getting at, but she seemed completely satisfied about it, whatever it was. The troubled frown faded from her face, and left it a serene ivory mask, as

expressionless as a magnolia petal. The two oblique
dark eyes that regarded mine were as limpid and
calm as a garden pool. I sometimes thought that
now and again a thought would flash through them
under the surface like a goldfish under the ferns,
but it never did. I had to agree with Lieutenant
Kelly that Gail Wyndham, with the motionless face
and full warm mouth and unfathomable eyes, might
do almost anything.

"Has Lieutenant Kelly talked to you, Gail?" I
asked as casually as I could.

"No, he hasn't. He was here about noon, and
asked for Eliot, but Eliot and Chase left a little
after nine, Estaphine said. He was here early too.
Estaphine thinks he's marvelous. He liked her
coffee."

"I think he's marvelous too," I said, "in his way.
I've promised to meet him at the Pennimans' at
two. I'm not sure just what for. I suspect it has to
do with the tablets of digitalin that were spilled on
the floor Tuesday."

"Was she actually poisoned with digitalin?"
Gail said, setting down her glass of milk. I didn't
get the impression that it was a point of absorbing
interest—just an inquiry.

"I haven't seen the pathologist's report," I said,
"but there doesn't seem to be any doubt of it."

"It's funny," she went on. "Of course, there are
other pills made out of digitalin, aren't there?"

"Many," I said.

"And you told me once it's possible to make an infusion of foxglove leaves and get the same thing. Or the same effect. Isn't it?"

"Yes. It's possible."

"Then why do they act as though those pills were the only ones in existence?"

"I don't suppose they do," I said. "But when people with a definite interest in somebody's death are where a lethal dose of a drug disappears, and that drug is later found to be in the stomach of the dead person, the evidence of cause and effect is very convincing. Isn't it?"

She entirely disregarded my question.

"Has anybody thought about John?" she asked. "The old Negro at the house? I doubt it."

"Then I think they ought to. He messes about with herbs. I used to eat the horehound candy he made. He doctors half the Negroes in town out of the herb garden by the Front Street wall."

I wondered if Lieutenant Kelly could have guessed whether Gail had a motive for turning suspicion towards old John. Somehow it didn't seem quite fair to me. It was too much like a mystery story in which you come to the last chapter and find that the third footman poisoned the duke's Bovril because he didn't like the color of his braces.

"There wouldn't be any point in that, would there?" I asked. "After all, they seemed to get on all right. He hasn't much to gain at his time of life. Anyway, that's stretching coincidence pretty far."

I was thinking about the little white pellet in the grass by the wall along Fleet Street. I couldn't make out whether Gail was unaware of that tell-tale evidence in the garden, or if she was confidently assuming no one else was aware of it. I was afraid that she took Lieutenant Kelly's obvious admiration and apparent good-will for innocence. But of course I didn't feel at liberty to enlighten her.

The most I felt I could allow myself to say was, "Lieutenant Kelly is a very thorough and extremely intelligent investigator." And I added, as we rose from the table, "I doubt if there's much that he misses."

"Then he'll find out who really did it," she said, following me into the living room. She lighted a cigarette and took a deep draught. Then she let the smoke drift slowly through her lips, and tossed the cigarette into the grate.

"You know, Aunt Ruth," she said, leaning forward, her elbows on her crossed knees, "I think Mr. Penniman is worried about Alice."

I thought with a little twinge of the great heart specialist.

"Any more than usual?" I said.

"I think so. He seems to be frightened to death that something's going to upset her. The servants are all talking about it. Even Nat noticed it. He said you'd think it was Alice that had gone off her nut and poisoned my ghastly old aunt."

I glanced at my watch.

"I wouldn't worry much about that," I said.

She smiled coolly at me, with even more than her usual sang-froid.

"Aunt Ruth," she said, "the maids are saying that Alice wasn't in her room Wednesday night."

"That's preposterous," I said, knowing very well that it wasn't at all. At the same moment the thought began running through my head that there was something behind Lieutenant Kelly's visit to the Pennimans that I hadn't thought of before.

"I'm going up there now, anyway. If your cousins come in, find out if they're going to be in for dinner, and tell Estaphine, will you please? Good-by."

"Good-by, Aunt Ruth."

I got my things and opened the front door. Gail was sitting where I'd left her, her open magazine on the floor, staring at the rug.

"Shall I tell Nat anything, if I see him?" I asked through the door.

"You won't see him," she answered dully, without glancing up. "He's gone to New York."

Lieutenant Kelly was calmly waiting for me, hat on the back of his head, cigar in the corner of his mouth, in my car parked in the drive.

"I thought you wouldn't mind taking me up," he said cheerfully, opening the door for me.

"Delighted," I said, glancing at him a little uneasily. He'd evidently been to the barber shop since I'd left him. His face had that white soft look that men never manage when they shave themselves, and he smelled like a barber shop too.

"You know," he went on, "I wanted to ask you a few things before I go up there. I was coming in, but I saw the girl by the window and thought I'd wait."

I wondered just how much of our conversation he might have overheard. I glanced across the garden to the house. Two of the windows in the living room were open on screens.

He followed my glance.

"I've been in the car all the time," he said.

I started the car. He took out a large silver watch from his vest pocket and examined it with pursed lips.

"It's twenty minutes to two," he decided. "Wonder if you'd like to drive me out to Stonehill before we go up. Stonehill," he repeated. "That's the place the two New Yorkers spent the evening, or that's their story."

"I have a call to make before I go to the Pennimans'," I said coldly.

"That's what your maid told me," he answered amiably. "But she said it was out the lake road. On the way to Stonehill, ain't it?"

I smiled in spite of myself.

"Check," I said, and let out the clutch.

"I'm not sure I like being seen with you," I remarked when we turned into Court House Square, causing a ripple of excitement in the knot of hangers-on and sitters-about that spend the time between meals—when any—waiting there for something to happen. "I'll be getting a reputation for dispensing poison to my patients. You've no notion how a rumor can become an established fact in this town."

Lieutenant Kelly's eyes crinkled.

"A fellow named Joe, at the pool hall, tells me odds are even on you, Judge Garth, and Mrs. Penniman," he remarked with heavy humor. "But no kidding, Doctor, I want you to give me the low-down on these Pennimans and the lunch they had. I hear it was a total loss."

All the humor had gone out of the lines around his eyes. I thought then that I wouldn't like to have Lieutenant Kelly after me. I suppose of course he's one of the reasons that Baltimore has the excellent police record it has.

"Well," I said, keeping an eye on him in one corner of the mirror over the windshield, "you've got to understand Mrs. Penniman. Old Miss Wyndham and her house have become an obsession with her in the last ten years. Mr. Penniman tried to buy the house when they first came down."

"From what they say in town he'd buy her the moon if she wanted it," said Lieutenant Kelly, with evident approval.

"And he'd probably manage," I added. "Miss

Wyndham's house is the only thing he's ever failed to get her."

"Failed so far," he said in a matter-of-fact way.

"He didn't understand how much a part of her the house was, and he certainly didn't know she had as much money as she had. Perhaps fifty thousand doesn't seem very much if you've got six million. Anyway, he came a bad cropper. Miss Wyndham never got over it, nor Alice either."

"True she said she'd burn the house down to keep this Penniman woman from getting it?"

"Yes. And I wouldn't put it beyond her, not for an instant."

Lieutenant Kelly was still meditating over that or other things when I drew up at the roadside in front of the Thorntons' place and reached for my bag.

"I'll be about ten minutes," I said, and left him trying to light a fresh cigar with the lighter on my dashboard that's been broken for three months.

I saw Mrs. Thornton and the twins, who seemed to be managing very nicely considering their extreme youth. This was their third day at their job, and their mother seemed much gratified at the way they slept.

I got back to my car just in time to hear Mr. Thornton, beaming, say, "You oughta hear them fellers holler!" He was standing there talking to Lieutenant Kelly.

Lieutenant Kelly slapped Mr. Thornton on the back.

"Twin boys!" he said. "Doctor, I'm going in to see them boys, and that's a fact."

With that he got out of the car, beaming at me and back at young Thornton, who's a quiet farmer and hardly ever sees anybody quite as grand as Lieutenant Kelly with his hat and his diamond ring.

They went in side by side. I waited about five minutes. At last they came out. Lieutenant Kelly's eyes were crinkled in a peculiar way, which I was just beginning to learn meant that he'd made a point.

"Here's ten bucks," he said to Thornton when they came down to the car, handing him a bill. "I want you to start a bank account for them young fellows. Put 'em through college. I got some of my own, but those fellows of yours got 'em beat six ways for Sunday. So long!"

"I'll be out to-morrow," I said. "Good-by."

When we had got a few hundred feet along the road I said, "How many sons have you got?" Anyone would have thought I felt he'd been keeping something very important from me.

"Not any," he said blandly. "But I got enough from that young fellow to knock Mr. Chase Wyndham into a cocked hat."

"So the ten dollars was in the nature of a bribe?"

"Not on your life. I tell a lie, and then I pay ten

bucks conscience money. Everybody's happy. Anyhow, they look as if they need it to pay the doctor's bill."

"I never charge for twins," I said. "It doesn't seem fair. Now, do you actually want to go to Stonehill Farm, or did I just bring you out to see Mr. Thornton?"

"We can go on, I guess, now we're this far," he said slyly. "I fixed your lighter, by the way."

We turned off the cement road into the cedar-lined avenue that runs a half mile or so before it turns sharply between the old gateposts of Stone-hill. We parked the car behind the cluster of small, whitewashed farm buildings and got out. Lieutenant Kelly had been there already, I gathered. He set out through the side gate and took the short cut through the hedge under the linden tree. We came out in front of the house. The garden stretched down from the front porch almost to the river. Great clusters of tawny and gold and rose chrysanthemums bloomed in it. A few zinnias were left, and some cosmos. Lieutenant Kelly picked a big yellow marigold and stuck it in his buttonhole.

"I like asters," he said simply.

We went up the grassy knoll and came to the wide low veranda. A couple of battered porch chairs were pulled forward to command a clear view of the water from under the cascades of wisteria and white jasmine leaves, interlaced with still blooming trumpet flowers.

Lieutenant Kelly pointed to the chair on the right.

"That's where Chase sat," he said, and went on to the question I'd have asked.

"I can tell because I found fifteen cigarette butts down here."

He pointed to the grass at the edge of the porch.

"He smoked all he had left in a package of Camels, and six Luckies."

"How do you know it was Chase?"

"And not the other fellow?"

I nodded.

"That's easy. Chase uses a lighter and I didn't find any matches. Eliot smokes a pipe and I found twenty-one burnt matches and no cigarettes down there. I guess you noticed he smokes Latakia? Well, it goes out all the time. But the point is like this. I watched that fellow Chase smoke twice now. He smokes half a cigarette in about three and a half minutes and lights another. You see? Well, now. Fifteen cigarettes takes him one hour. At the outside, Doctor. Now. That's an hour of smoking. *But*—he and brother Eliot killed a pint bottle of Scotch!"

"Rye," I said. "Maryland rye."

"All right, rye. The bottle says Bourbon, as a matter of fact. It's just as likely to have been one as the other."

I agreed.

"Now then," he went on. "You get the point.

You can't tell me a pint of licker and fifteen cigarettes kept that fellow sitting here three hours, sitting in the moonlight and talking about old times.
Remember this too: his brother says he was in a
nervous state."

"He wasn't talking about old times entirely," I
said. "He was telling his brother about his business
troubles."

"Sure," said Lieutenant Kelly. "And he was getting more and more worked up—with the help of
the bottle. Ever drink a pint of whiskey minus one
drink?"

I assured him I had not.

"Well, you feel it. Especially if you're in a nervous state, and more particularly if you put it
down in one hour."

"But they both say they were here three hours,"
I objected.

He nodded calmly.

"That's just what we're doing," he said. "We're
checking up on *that*. Now I know either he didn't
come here at nine, or he left before twelve. Or
both. And your friend Thornton was sitting on his
front porch, waiting to put in a call to you any
minute for the late interesting event, at five minutes past eleven, and he sees a big sports car with
two men in it and a New York license plate on the
back, going hell bent for leather past his place,
towards town."

I was silent a minute.

"There wasn't a woman with them," I said.

He shook his head.

"No," he said. "The fellow that runs the camera at the movie on Calvert Street saw her about that time on his way home. She was running into Fleet Street, alone, at half-past eleven. Say, we'd ought to be going along to the Pennimans', I guess."

CHAPTER

14

I DON'T know how much of what finally turned out to be true Lieutenant Kelly knew at this point. I've accused him since of pretending to know a whole lot more than he really did. He assumes, on such an occasion, an expression that is what I imagine a composite photograph of Mona Lisa and the Sphinx would have, and says something about knowing how and when to take the jumps. He certainly acted as if he had the whole thing sewed up tight, as he himself put it. Having no reputation as a lieutenant of detectives to uphold, I'm quite willing to admit that I was totally bewildered by the whole affair. Although at this point even I really had nearly all the essential clues in my hands.

Lieutenant Kelly's method of bringing up each person who'd been involved at any point in the affair, and proving conclusively, as far as I was concerned, that that person could easily have done it and undoubtedly did, confused me no end. Especially when half an hour later he tacitly denied that he'd ever remotely considered such a possibility.

The four obvious major questions I was com-

pletely at a loss about, when we left Stonehill
Farm.

First, who had given old Miss Nettie the poison
dose of digitalin?

Second, who had stolen her will?

Third, who had stolen the jewels?

Fourth, who was writing the poison-pen letters
to Gail?

It is, I suppose, a truism that people don't normally commit crime unless they have something to
gain by so doing. I'd already examined my four
points from that angle, but I went over them again
as we turned onto the paved road and started back
to town.

First, I thought, Gail and her two cousins were
the only people who could gain anything by the loss
of the will. They each gain approximately $60,000.
There was, of course, the remote possibility of Mrs.
Penniman's being helped to get the house, if it now
had to be sold. There was furthermore the idea that
Richard Wyndham had taken the will, fearing that
the old woman might really burn down the house.
Having heard his bitter accusation of Daphne Lake
in the cellars of Wyndham House, I thought I
could dismiss that.

Second, the value of the jewels was not great, and
it would be hard to sell them. Was it true that
Daphne Lake was a small-time jewel thief? It
seemed hard to believe.

The third point was a little different. It seems

safe to say that anyone who writes poison-pen letters is definitely unbalanced; so that, unless we
were dealing with someone unbelievably malicious
and far-seeing, it was not immediately related to
our problem. Except, of course, in so far as there
was no truth in their accusations. That of course is
the terrible thing about such letters. They so often
contain a grain of bitter truth. I couldn't, however,
at the time see that anyone had much to gain by
writing such letters, unless of course they were also
writing them to the police.

Fourth, five people gained by the death of Miss
Nettie Wyndham. That fact was certain. I ticked
them off on mental fingers.

Richard Wyndham as sole legatee, or as heir to
one-fourth the estate if the will did not turn up.

Chase, Eliot and Gail, only in case the will did
not turn up. If it was not destroyed, they gained
nothing.

Mrs. Penniman, because she now probably had a
chance to buy the house.

That as far as I could see it, was where we stood.
I had to admit that it left a good deal to be
accounted for. For example, Daphne Lake. Had
she stolen the will, as Richard Wyndham seemed
certain? If so, for what purpose?

I should have liked to put these questions to
Lieutenant Kelly, but he sat beside me with an air
so cocksure that I held my peace. At least I did

until he turned to me with the remark, "Would you say, Doctor, that Mrs. Penniman is a little batty?"

I have of course often said that Alice Penniman is as crazy as a loon, and meant it. But that was either to Alice, her husband, or her social secretary. Certainly not to a detective.

"Don't be absurd," I said.

"They tell me she's neurotic," he said calmly. "Mr. Taylor said so himself."

"I didn't know he knew the word," I said. "Besides, being neurotic doesn't mean you're insane. Women like Mrs. Penniman, and of her age, frequently show a lack of balance, and certain morbid characteristics. Nevertheless, they're perfectly sane."

"Meaning you don't think she'd go down and poison the old girl to keep her from burning the house down."

"I mean just that. In the first place she couldn't have made the trip down the hill, much less got over a wall and into the house. I saw her the next morning and she was still a sick woman."

"Yeah," he said. "But she does queer things once in a while, don't she?"

"Oh, yes. I'll admit that."

We turned in the gates of the Penniman estate, and in a few minutes were seated precariously on Alice's fragile gold chairs in her Louis Quinze drawing-room. Lieutenant Kelly was excessively ill at ease. The lounge at the Elks' Club was his period.

Fortunately we didn't have to sit there long. I went across the hall and got Samuel Penniman and told him he'd better stand by in case Lieutenant Kelly pressed Alice too far. He came back with me, and I introduced him to the detective.

Samuel Penniman and Lieutenant Kelly were made for different levels, perhaps, but certainly in the same social order, and they recognized that at once. Samuel understood Lieutenant Kelly; Lieutenant Kelly understood Samuel. They agreed on the Democratic Party, and I dare say would have on nine other views out of ten. In fact they got on so well that I was on the point of leaving when Lieutenant Kelly announced that his sole purpose in disturbing the Pennimans was to see the room in which Miss Nettie had been received after the unveiling. He had no intention, he said, of bothering Mrs. Penniman at all. This wasn't anything for a lady to be mixed up in.

Samuel promptly led the way across the hall to the long drawing-room, furnished in the fine old pieces of Chippendale and Phyfe that were to fill in, some day, the bare spots in Wyndham House. Lieutenant Kelly surveyed the room with pursed lips and a cocked eye.

"Well, well," he said. "Now then, let's just see whereabouts everybody was standing here that day. What's your idea of it, Mr. Penniman?"

Samuel thought a moment.

"The old woman sat here," he said, pointing to

the green Chippendale fireside chair. "Richard Wyndham was standing on that side of her. My wife was on this side. Judge Garth and Gail were over there. Ruth, where were you?"

"By the table," I said.

"And my son and I were down there by the window talking to Chase and Eliot Wyndham," he continued. I was amazed that he remembered all of it as well as he did.

"My wife collapsed when that old woman began carrying on like a maniac. We'd all got more or less into a circle by that time. Ruth here—Dr. Fisher—ran to my wife and told my son to bring her her bag off the hall table."

Samuel pulled out his handkerchief and mopped a very sparsely thatched pink cranium.

"I was terribly alarmed," he went on. Lieutenant Kelly clucked sympathetically.

"Every time she has one of those attacks I think she's gone. They've been more frequent lately. Well, Ruth gave her one of those pills to revive her heart, or whatever it does. Then we got her upstairs."

"Who went out of the room with you?"

"Dr. Fisher here, my son and myself. The rest stayed behind. When we came down, Richard Wyndham had taken the old woman away. Chase and Eliot Wyndham left after a short time. Then Judge Garth and Gail Wyndham."

"Now then," said Lieutenant Kelly. "Had you

found out the pills were missing before they left, or after they left?"

He kept doing all sorts of odd things with his face during Samuel's recital, twisting it up and pulling it back into place, rubbing his nose and scratching the under part of his chin. I learned later that that meant he was getting a great idea. He told me so himself.

"After," Samuel said.

"So none of 'em knew you knew the pills was gone."

"They knew they'd been spilled all over the floor."

"Oh, sure," said Lieutenant Kelly. "I got that. Now, who called attention to the fact that they was gone?"

Samuel and I looked at each other.

"Nat, wasn't it?" I said.

"Yes. I believe it was Nat," he agreed.

"He picked 'em up and put 'em on the table, they say."

"Seven of them," I replied. "The bottle had twelve in it. I used one. There were two that weren't shaken out of it."

"And Nat found two on the floor later on," Samuel added.

"Well, well," said Lieutenant Kelly. "Now then. Was anything said about it being digitalin and therefore poison."

"I don't think so," I said.

Samuel shook his head. "I agree with Dr. Fisher. But I was pretty much excited. Then later I was out of the room."

Lieutenant Kelly nodded. He seemed to be thinking hard about something, so that quite a long silence ensued. Samuel pulled a cigar out of his pocket and handed it to him. Lieutenant Kelly said, "Thanks," smelled it, put it in his pocket and took out one of his own.

"Well now," he said. "I understand you've made arrangements to buy the house, now the old woman's dead."

He lighted his cigar with an obviously false air of disinterest. I was beginning to recognize his little tricks, and I thought I could see that this was nothing but a shot in the dark. If it was it worked perfectly. Samuel flushed angrily.

"Nothing definite at all," he said shortly. "I took the matter up with Chase Wyndham as a mere formality."

Lieutenant Kelly blinked innocently.

"Sure," he said. "That's what I meant. How much did that option cost you, now?"

"It was in no sense an option," Mr. Penniman replied, plainly very much ruffled. "It was in the nature of a . . ."

"A consideration?" Lieutenant Kelly suggested.

"Of a consideration. Chase Wyndham agreed to persuade the other three heirs to sell me the house. It's entirely in the open."

"Sure," Lieutenant Kelly said again. "Of course, though, if the others won't do it, he can hold up anything they decide on. I guess then it would have to come up to public auction."

A dull apoplectic flush darkened Samuel Penniman's pink well-fed face and spread up over his bald head. The veins in his temples swelled angrily.

"No such course was suggested for an instant," he said hotly. "I've offered a hundred thousand for the damn house. I'll pay two hundred thousand if I have to."

Lieutenant Kelly stared in admiration at him.

"Jeez," he said simply. "Well, I hope you don't have to. You going downtown now, Doctor? If you are I'll trouble you for a lift."

"The trouble with women," he remarked as we slipped from under the Pennimans' porte-cochère, "is that they jump to conclusions."

"Wrong," I said. "What conclusion have I jumped to?"

"You jumped to one right then," he said, the wrinkles around his eyes deepening with great good humor. "I wasn't talking about you. It's Mrs. Penniman I was thinking about."

"Well," I said, "what's she jumped to?"

"She thinks her old man poisoned the old lady to get the house for her."

"Sam Penniman poison Miss Wyndham!" I exclaimed, almost running off the road.

"Sure. He's got everything anybody else has got. Motive—that wife of his wants the house. She's going to have those fits if she doesn't get it. He's damned if he don't get it for her. Opportunity— well, he could have got hold of those pills easy as anybody else there. Nothing so far-fetched about it, when you get down to it."

I shook my head.

"No," I said positively. "It leaves too many things unexplained. The will for instance. There's no point in it."

"Yeah?" he said. "We got to see about that. We got to go into the business of the fellow Richard Wyndham. What if he'd refused to sell to Penni-man? What if Penniman went there, poisoned the old lady, saw the will and says, 'Now then, here's my son going to marry this jane, he might as well get sixty thousand. It's hers by rights.'"

"Mr. Penniman," I said, "is worth at least six million."

He nodded.

"That's just the kind that don't throw away sixty grand," he said, and I've no doubt he was right.

"Look here, Doctor," he went on. "You told me yourself Penniman'd do anything for that woman. Is that right or is it baloney?"

"No. I think it's right."

"He's just that kind of animal."

"Yes. He's just that kind."

"Son like him?"

"Nat? Rather."

"I guess he'd do anything for that girl."

"Maybe."

He shrugged his broad shoulders.

"Not so much fun for him to sit around and see her treated the way the old woman treated her," he said placidly.

"I imagine it was pretty hard."

"I'll say it was. Say, Doctor, you can leave me off here at the Court House. I got to see Taylor."

Lieutenant Kelly had not bothered to explain how he knew Alice Penniman thought Samuel had murdered old Miss Nettie. In the couple of blocks between the Court House where I'd dropped him and my home I concluded, on going over it, that he was—to put it plainly—pulling my leg. So I dismissed the matter. It was therefore something of a shock when I opened my front door and saw Alice Penniman sitting on the sofa in the living room, crying. Her face was drawn and her eyes had that staring hunted look that I see so often in people who are almost beside themselves with anxiety and fear.

She didn't say anything when I came in, put my bag on the table and took off my hat.

I almost said, "Well, now," but caught myself in time.

Instead I said, "Pull yourself together, Alice," and realized from the tinge of asperity in my voice that I was pretty near the ragged edge myself and ought to take some of my own advice.

"How about some tea, or a glass of sherry?" I said, and rang for Estaphine.

"Miss Gail done lef' yo' this yere," Estaphine said primly when she came in, and handed me an envelope addressed in pencil: "Aunt Ruth." I opened it, read it, and glanced at Alice, who was as forlorn and miserable a looking object as I'd seen for some time. She'd simply caved in. I glanced back at the note in my hand.

"Dear Aunt Ruth,

"I don't think you really believe I had anything to do with my aunt's death or the will. I didn't, really. But I've decided to marry Nat anyway. He's waiting for me in Baltimore. I'm taking the Ford. You might tell Mrs. Penniman it's just too bad. We'll be home Monday. Love and thanks!

"Gail."

I drank a cup of tea and handed the letter to Alice.

She took it listlessly, read it, and started to cry again.

"Oh Ruth," she moaned, "it's so terrible! Why did they do it?"

She wrung her hands tragically and dabbed at her eyes with a useless wet little wad of linen and lace. I said nothing. I've known Alice and her spells long enough to know that shortly she'd out with it, and in half an hour be herself again.

"Don't tell me you don't know Samuel did this terrible thing," she cried. "It's all my fault,—my greed and my vanity! Oh yes it is! I know it, I've wanted that house and nothing else would do. When she said she was going to burn it I could see Sam getting simply wild. Oh Ruth, it's terrible, terrible!"

She broke into a fresh spasm of tears. I poured myself another cup of tea and waited.

"I got up that night and went in Sam's room to tell him something, about eleven o'clock, and he was gone. I went downstairs and he wasn't there. I almost died, Ruth! I'd known he was going to do it from the moment he said she ought to be shot for acting that way. Then I tried to go upstairs and I just couldn't make it, so I turned off the lights and sat down in the chair by the fireplace and wrapped Sam's rug around me. I must have gone to sleep because all of a sudden I heard voices, and Sam and Nat came in."

I put down my tea cup. Her voice had sunk almost to a whisper, her eyes dilated with remembered horror.

"Sam put something down on the table and said, 'Well, we won't have any more trouble with her.'"

She had stopped crying now.

"Yes?" I said. "What did you do?"

"I just waited until they went upstairs, and then

I got up, and went to bed. Oh, I knew, don't you see? I knew what they'd done just as well as if they'd told me!"

I listened to this with a sinking heart, and tried to combat uneasiness with common sense. Alice was looking at me, waiting, I knew, for some sort of reassurance.

"For Heaven's sake, Alice!" I said. "Don't you see how many things could have happened? That doesn't mean that your men went out and murdered that old woman. It's a hundred to one they were out doctoring some wretched animal. You've got brood mares and Lord knows what on the farm."

She shook her head.

"No, Ruth," she said, with a sort of self-pity, "it's that house. It's a millstone around my neck. And that's what I wanted to tell Sam."

"That the house was a millstone?" I asked caustically. "Sam's known that for a good many years."

"No, Ruth," she said. "Not that. What I wanted to tell Samuel was that I don't want that house. I waked up suddenly that night and realized that I didn't. I really don't, at all."

"Lieutenant Kelly," I said, "was right."

By this time she had, as usual, become almost normally brisk.

"About what?" she demanded.

"About women," I replied.

Several people were waiting in my office when I finally argued Alice into going back home and talking the whole matter over with Samuel—including the marriage of their son. A child with a fractured arm from indiscreet roller-skating, a woman with a pain under the arm from not enough to occupy her mind otherwise, a man with a bad case of poison ivy from ignorance of botany, occupied my next hour. I had just put away my last record card when the telephone rang and I recognized the frantic voice of Mr. Thornton.

His wife, he said, had been took real bad. He described symptoms that I knew might be either quite alarming or the product of over-wrought nerves. I told him I'd be there in eight minutes—which is pretty fast driving from my house to his farm—and snatched my bag and hat. As it turned out, I was very glad I'd gone, though not on account of Mrs. Thornton, who turned out to be suffering from far too much of her husband's mother and maiden aunt.

I left their place about six o'clock, just at dusk. It's always lovely in Maryland in the autumn evenings. I was driving back rather slowly—about thirty, I imagine—along the county road, thinking about Alice and Gail and Lieutenant Kelly, when I noticed, without being particularly interested in it, an open car parked by the side of the road. It isn't an uncommon occurrence, and I should have passed it without a thought, if I hadn't seen a bright head barely showing above the folded top.

I was interested then in spite of myself. I was even more so when I glanced at the license plate and saw that the car was from New York. They must have heard my car coming, or seen it in the mirror, because the yellow head ducked down out of sight as I went by. The man in the car looked coolly at me. I recognized him vaguely, but I couldn't place him.

I went a little faster, racking my brain to think where I'd seen that man before. It was no use, but I couldn't get him out of my head.

I heard my name called as I went around Court House Square, and saw my friend Lieutenant Kelly disengage himself from a group by the fence and step out into the street.

"I've been out to the Thorntons'," I said before he could say anything.

"You got some evidence?" he asked jocularly.

"Plenty," I said. "Chiefly our lady with the yellow hair sitting in a New York car with an unknown stranger along the roadside."

The good-humor went out of Lieutenant Kelly's face like a flash.

"Yeah?" he said. "Well, well. I'll be seeing you, Doc."

I left him heading rapidly for a car in front of the Court House.

I was just sitting down to dinner when the door bell rang.

"It's that police detective man from Balt'mur," said Estaphine, her old eyes fairly popping out of her head.

"Show him in."

Lieutenant Kelly's manner was more offensively confidential than ever, and more offensively self-confident too.

"Thought you might like to see something pretty, Doc," he said. He set the brown holland bag he carried on the dinner table, untied the black shoe string around the top, and turned it bottom up.

"Aha!", he said very soberly, like a conjurer who's just finished a very good trick, but one that ought to have been expected of him.

On my table were several rings, a short string of pearls, and a gleaming silver coffee pot.

"Lake and the boy-friend handed 'em over," he said, with a wink even more jocular than usual.

Estaphine's eyes bulged, but she didn't forget her social training.

"Would yo' all like some dinnah, Captain?" she said.

"I sure would—if the madam don't mind."

"Not at all," I said.

CHAPTER

15

LIEUTENANT KELLY maintained an obstinate good-natured silence on the entire matter of the Wyndham jewels. There was a general rumor in town that they'd turned up, but there's no doubt it started in my kitchen. Estaphine was as proud of having the Baltimore police detective come to the house as if he'd been the governor.

I saw quite a little of him off and on in the next few days, and found him singularly communicative on every subject but the Wyndham case. The only actually new bit of information I got came from another source. I called up the Patch Box Saturday afternoon for a manicure and found that Daphne Lake was no longer connected with the shop. That very day I met the woman whose house the girl lived in. She raised her brows significantly. Miss Lake had left her house late Friday evening, bag and baggage. She didn't say where she was going, but her landlady hadn't been able to avoid seeing the car, with a man in it, that was waiting for her around the corner.

Chase and Eliot were still at my house. I saw

very little of them, however, as I was pretty busy going in and out, taking my meals whenever I happened to have time. I was at the Pennimans' for dinner Sunday in the middle of the day. They both seemed a little more at peace, but it was a dismal meal. The Wyndham affair wasn't so much as mentioned.

On Monday about noon I was in my office when Gail and Nat arrived. The Wyndham case certainly simply didn't exist for either of them—in fact, nothing much else seemed to, except themselves. They were for the moment in that sublime egocentric state that middle age finds so disconcerting.

"We met cousin Richard," Gail said, when the business of receiving them back home was finished. "He said he's meeting Chase and Eliot here at three o'clock to-day to talk over the division of the property. I'm supposed to be here too."

"You stay away," Nat ordered, putting an absurdly protective arm around her. "You're not interested in that."

"I'm not?" she said quickly. "If you think I'm letting them say what's to be done and what isn't you're crazy."

I'd often reflected that Nat's training with his mother ought to make him the ideal husband for a Wyndham.

He shrugged his shoulders.

"Okay, old dear," he said. But he wasn't very happy about it.

Lieutenant Kelly came around about two o'clock. For the first time in my experience with him he looked a little worn. He took off his hat and sat down in my office with something very near a groan.

"Anything wrong," I asked.

"Anything right, would be nearer it," he replied, running his hand through his thick gray hair.

"I suppose of course you know the heirs are meeting this afternoon," I remarked after a few minutes of silence, during which he stared at the ceiling.

He pulled himself into a sitting posture, and looked at me with evident dissatisfaction.

"Yeah," he said. "To divide the swag. Well, now, that's what we been waiting for. The sooner the quicker."

"What do you mean?"

"Nothing much," he said with a wink. "This here meeting this afternoon oughta settle some points. It won't be long now. Taylor's been raring to go for a week. He's got a water-tight case. Point number two, his term ends pretty soon. You see what that means?"

"I suppose you mean he's got to get a conviction."

"Sure. Got to, and going to. Believe me, there'll be a different brand of justice around here next year, if he gets in again."

I looked inquiringly at him.

"Judge Garth goes out this year. He's three years

past retirement now. Without him sitting on Taylor, see?—there'll be no holding him."

"I see," I said. "I guess you're right."

That brought him nearly to himself.

"Right?" he said. "Sure I'm right. He'll get the conviction. Murdering the last of the old aristocrats."

He looked nevertheless very much dissatisfied with things.

"Look here, Lieutenant Kelly," I said. "I want to know what part Richard Wyndham's played in this business."

He gave me a most sardonic look.

"You do?" he said. "Lady, I'll tell you a little secret. So would a lot of other people. Including yours truly."

"Don't tell me there's something about this business you don't know."

"There's a lot of things I don't know, and there's a couple I do. For instance. I know why Miss Lake couldn't get him on the phone after you came up from the cellar."

"Why?"

"Because she didn't try."

"But I heard her."

"But you didn't see she had the receiver still on the hook, did you?"

"No, I didn't."

"She did."

"How do you know?"

"She told me. You know why? She didn't call up then because she knew he wasn't home."

"Where was he?" I demanded.

"In the cellar. He'd just cracked you over the arm, and Lake knew it. She waited until he'd had time to get home before she called up. She didn't want anybody telling him the phone was ringing while he was out."

"Did she know what he was after?"

He looked at me in surprise.

"You're asking me that? Didn't you have a ring-side seat when he caught her with the goods?"

"Well," I said, "I can see what she was after, but I can't make sense to his being down there."

"I'll tell you about that too," Lieutenant Kelly said in his most kindly manner. "You saw him lock her in the cellar Tuesday afternoon, just after the great luncheon party."

"You said it was Gail down there," I said, vexed.

"That's what *you* thought," he returned with a grin. "I didn't say it. That was Lake. She wasn't at the beauty parlor that afternoon. She was around that Wyndham place all the time. Then she got herself asked back for the night."

He took out a cigar, bit the end off, and spat it into my wastebasket.

"Well, now," he said. "Richard Wyndham figured there was something down there she wanted. He beat her to it."

He lighted the cigar, and gave me a confiding wink.

"He'd been suspecting there was something phoney about her for a while. Or that's his story. Says he got on to it by the way she talked. When she'd get serious, he says, she'd talk real proper English, like a lady, and then she'd remember and throw in a lot of slang. So he decides he'll just see. So he locked her in. But she got out—remember that little window? When he went back, after you and the judge had gone home, he could see how she'd done it."

"Didn't she know we were all upstairs?" I said. "You can hear people walking about."

"Not till it was too late, so she took a chance. You see, she figured you'd be at the Pennimans' until three. Well, the old dame came home at half-past one and she was caught. She couldn't get out. She got in the cellar and decides to stay.

"Now, then. Richard knew she was in the house, so he goes over—this is *his* story—and parks outside in the garden, waiting for something to happen. He saw plenty, or that's what he says. He saw her going around with a light from room to room. Saw the light through the shutters."

"You can't see a light through those shutters," I said.

"You can in back. I had a fellow with a flash in there last night. I saw a twinkle every little while."

"But Miss Lake didn't have a flash," I said. "She had an oil lamp burning, when I met her."

"Her battery burned out about eleven-thirty. She had the light in her pocket when you saw her. That's one of the reasons she called you over. Well, anyhow, Richard gets in the house about eleven. He figures she hadn't got to the cellar, but she'd get there sooner or later, and he'd find out what she's up to. Well, when he gets there, or while he's down there, suddenly he gets a great idea. He's acting on it when something happens upstairs and he hears Miss Lake on the phone calling you up."

"What happened upstairs?" I said.

Lieutenant Kelly was perversely mysterious.

"My mother used to tell me," he said grinning, "that's for me to know and you to find out."

He blew a perfect circle of smoke up to the ceiling and nodded in great satisfaction.

"Well, now," he went on. "He's just getting under way with the great idea when you and Lake come downstairs. He figures you'd caught him, and he doesn't want to get caught. He hides around that big pillar, and cracks you over the arm so's you'd drop the flash, and out he gets. When Lake phoned him he'd just got in."

I thought all that over.

"He didn't know his aunt was dead, then?" I asked.

"That's his story."

"He was around the house when Judge Garth

and I were there, and after we left until Miss Lake came," I said. "Was he the last person to see her alive?"

"Nope. Lake saw her."

"He was at the Pennimans'," I went on. "He had plenty of opportunity to put the pills in the water. I suppose the only thing he lacks is motive."

A superior smile spread over Lieutenant Kelly's lanky features, and his eyes crinkled more than I'd ever seen them before.

"Motive and then some," he said. "That young fellow has more debts than anybody in this town, and he's borrowed more money on the strength of the old lady's will than you'd think people'd be foolish enough to pass out. And say, he was one scared guy when the old dame sent for the judge and told him to get out of the room. I've got the word of a dozen cronies of his that he said more'n once he hoped the old girl'd pass in before she changed that will."

I shook my head.

"That doesn't sound very good, Lieutenant," I said. "His aunt knew what he was like. Anyway, that doesn't explain why he took the will."

"He says he was going to take the will, but when he goes around for it after you left that night, it's gone."

"How did he get in? Dr. Michaels locked the door."

"That's easy. Those old locks are all the same. Any key in the house fits any of 'em."

"So he thinks Daphne Lake took it."

"Nope," said Lieutenant Kelly. "Wrong again, Doc. He thinks she tried for it but didn't get it, see? That's why he goes back the next night to see what's up. Then's when he saw her come through the gate and go around back of the house. He figures then she'd make a bee line for the cellar, so he gets there first. That's when you saw them."

I nodded.

"Daphne seemed to know right where to go," I said.

"I'll say she did. And I'll say for her she got it right from the beginning."

"Well," I said patiently, "who's the man I saw her with Friday night?"

"The same fellow you saw her signaling to that night. You and the young fellow across the street. He's from New York. Guess he's been working with her from the beginning. They tell me he's been in town, off and on for six months."

And that was very odd. I knew I'd seen him before somewhere. I remembered now. He had been in town for a few days just before Daphne Lake came; I remembered seeing him two or three times, standing around with the other loafers in Court House Square. I'd not seen him since. Somehow the idea of Daphne Lake's being a member of a gang of crooks was very disconcerting. I realized how, under proper

or improper conditions, it could have been Gail, or
any number of intelligent young girls around. I suppose it's a matter of circumstance mostly. And I
remembered that I'd often thought of Daphne Lake
as being much too intelligent for the job she had.
If that was really her business she'd have owned
the shop.

"Have you got her?"

"She's in New York. We know where to find her
when he want her."

"Well, now," Lieutenant Kelly added, "it's
about time for 'em to show up."

He examined his large silver watch.

"Are you going to be present?" I said, surprised.

He gave me a very pleasant wink.

"Not that anybody but you knows about," he
said. "Both you and me are going to be here, listening. I got to know what it's all about, and I got to
have a witness to it."

I shook my head decisively.

"No, indeed," I said. "That's not my business."

"Say, Doc," he said, "it's your business to look
out for that ward of yours's interests. And she's
going to need it. And if you don't do it I don't know
who will."

We compromised on the arrangement that Lieutenant Kelly could stay in concealment in my office,
and that I would indicate to Gail my willingness to
be present if she wanted me to. The situation—from
Lieutenant Kelly's point of view—was made easier

by the fact that when Gail came, with Chase and Eliot, she herself asked me to be present at the meeting. So the four of us went into the living room, and in a few minutes we were joined by Richard Wyndham and a man whom I knew only by reputation, which was not very good. He's a lawyer in town, and as unscrupulous as if he lived in a much larger place.

It was a curious gathering. Chase Wyndham opened the discussion, when we were all seated in a strange mutual suspicion, I suppose, around the living room. He didn't, he said, need to say they regretted their aunt's death, because he saw no necessity for such hypocrisy. He did, however, feel that it was unfortunate she had died as she did. He proceeded to say that inasmuch as their aunt had died intestate, he felt that they should and must come to a friendly disposition of her property.

I noticed Richard's lawyer clear his throat, and shift his crossed legs, encased in the most pressed and striped trousers I've seen for a long time.

Chase noticed it too, and appeared rather annoyed, I thought.

"I was under the impression," he said caustically, "that we were all gentlemen, and could settle this matter as such."

Richard Wyndham's smile was purposely exasperating.

"Since I'm the only one who's got anything to

lose," he said coolly, "it seems fair enough that I should be represented professionally."

Chase's lean dark face flushed angrily. Eliot looked at him with a warning shake of the head, and Chase appeared to be trying to keep control of himself. It was interesting to see the three Wyndham men together and see the difference their lives had made in them and in their appearance. Each had the Wyndham dark wavy hair, touched with gray at the temples. Richard's and Chase's was smoothly and sleekly combed. Eliot's was parted most any way. Richard's face was confidently mocking and supercilious, Chase's drawn, with lines around his eyes and mouth that came from worry and too hard a pace. Eliot's face had a definitely spiritual quality that the others lacked. It was easy to see that his life had been very different from theirs. All in all, I thought, he was certainly a much pleasanter person.

I glanced from them to Gail, who was very like them all, in a way. Her face was what a softened, delicate ivory mask of theirs might be. She seemed entirely untroubled by the tense antagonism of the others. Once I saw her and Eliot exchange glances, but the perfect magnolia quality of her face remained unchanged.

Chase Wyndham made a definite effort to stay composed.

"My brother and I feel," he said, "that it would be unwise in the present state of the market to attempt to liquidate a large part of Aunt Nettie's securities, or her real property, with the exception, possibly, of the house."

The lawyer moved in his chair again, and smiled unpleasantly. Richard's upper lip curled ever so slightly. Gail's waxen pallor deepened perceptibly.

"Mr. Penniman," he went on, with a faint tinge of what I thought was defiance in his voice, "has offered $100,000 for the house, and $25,000 for its contents. I don't know what you think about that, Gail, or you, Richard; but that seems a pretty good figure to Eliot and me. Especially as things are at present. I think we could have got more for it, of course, in 1928. But those days are gone forever."

He smiled uneasily. No one else moved a muscle.

"Inasmuch as Gail has now married a Penniman, I think it's fitting that the house goes along with her."

Chase must have been aware of the growing hostility in the atmosphere, but I must say he carried it off very well.

"What do you say, Gail?" he added.

Her reply surprised me a little.

"Mr. Penniman will pay more than $25,000 for the furniture," she said curtly.

Her three cousins looked at her in astonishment. I was sorry the lawyer was there. In the morning it would be all over town that she'd married Nat for his money, and was willing to make the asbestos man pay through the nose.

"What I mean is," she added quickly, "that if we

can sell the furniture for more than that, there's no reason why we shouldn't. After all, I don't expect you people to just hand me five or ten thousand."

I suspect that was the first time that Richard Wyndham had felt any actual kinship with his cousin Gail. He smiled quickly at her.

"Of course," Chase said in some annoyance, "we'll get as much for it as we can. What do you say, Richard. Or does this fellow here do your talking for you?"

Richard smiled maliciously.

"My client," the lawyer said, "has nothing to say at this time. Except possibly to remind you, sir, that it has not yet been determined what happened to Miss Wyndham's will. We are prepared to wait until we feel it possible to speak with some certainty."

Chase glanced at Eliot, who had got up and was standing in the middle of the room.

"In that case," he said quietly, "we're simply wasting everybody's time. We'll have our attorneys meet you whenever you wish."

It turned out, however, that that was a little previous. Richard and his lawyer left almost at once. Gail went upstairs to get some of her things. Eliot and I were standing by the fireplace talking, and Chase had not moved except to light a cigarette. There was a preoccupied and very worried look on his face.

Then I heard the door of my office open. Lieutenant Kelly came across the hall into the living room.

He walked directly up to Chase Wyndham and touched him on the shoulder. "Mr. Wyndham," he said, "I've got a warrant for your arrest."

Chase turned the color of putty. His mouth opened twice, but no sound came from it.

Lieutenant Kelly answered the question he could not ask.

"I'm arresting you," he said stolidly, "for the murder of Miss Antoinette Wyndham."

CHAPTER

16

I SUPPOSE nearly everybody in the county was in Court House Square the morning of November 1st, when the Wyndham trial opened. I saw Frank Lazenby, of Lazenby's The Ladies Store, who's foreman of the grand jury that indicted Chase Wyndham, come through the crowded area, saluting his friends and discreetly spitting tobacco juice at the pedestal of the Civil War group at the corner of the Square. No one took that as in any way a gesture of contempt or familiarity. It was practically the only clear space in the Square, except for the Revolutionary group in the center. The necessary by-products of tobacco are my chief objection to it, as a matter of fact, and I was perfectly aware that Frank Lazenby and his tobacco juice aren't any worse than Lieutenant Kelly and his sodden mangled cigar ends that I'd got used to knocking off my tables or chair rails after every visit.

Frank Lazenby went up the Court House steps and turned around obligingly—"giving the newspaper men a break," remarked Nat Penniman, who had come with me and was shoving me by the elbow into the little wake left by Mr. Lazenby.

The wide wooden stairs leading up to Judge Garth's courtroom were packed with people who still thought they might get in. They fell back a little for Mr. Lazenby, and a little fire of greetings moved steadily in front of us.

"Hi, Frank."

"Hi, boy."

"Mornin', Mr. Lazenby."

I suppose some of them hoped possibly, through Mr. Lazenby's offices, to get inside the green baize doors, each with its small round window, that the bailiff guarded inexorably.

As we came up he greeted us with professional and tried affability.

"Mornin', Mr. Lazenby. Mornin', Doctor. Mornin', sir."

He opened the door and waved us in. Mr. Lazenby entered with the importance to which his position entitled him, went to the place reserved for the jury panel, and shook hands with each of the nineteen men who had preceded him to their seats. Nat and I took places near the back of the room, which was already fairly crowded, and looked about. I knew most of the people there, especially those, twelve of whom were to make up the jury that would try Chase Wyndham. I wondered how much chance he had against the combined forces of Lieutenant Kelly and Mr. Weems Taylor and any twelve of that crowd. Not that they aren't many of them very excellent men; but they aren't like Chase Wyndham.

Nat had evidently been looking them over too. He leaned closer to me and whispered, "As if every damn one of 'em hadn't made up his mind the day after it happened."

It was true, of course. The murder of Miss Nettie and the loss of the will and the jewels had turned the town practically inside out. Miss Nettie was known with that peculiar intimacy with which people know an almost legendary figure in a town. Nothing she said or ate was secret to them. Each new example of her tyranny of wealth and meanness brought vigorous and resentful protest. But now by the always curious alchemy of death they remembered a pathetic old woman and an aged devoted dog hobbling in the magnolia-scented dusk to the corner post-box. They remembered that she'd given the Civil War group that I've just mentioned in connection with Mr. Lazenby. They remembered how she had loved her nephew Richard, and how devoted he was to her. So they shook their heads and agreed generally that Chase was and had always been a bad lot. It was what you'd rightfully expect from a young fellow who'd sold the home farm, gone to the city, and got up to his neck in debts.

I suppose the one thing you couldn't say about any man in town was that he had an open mind in

the case of the State of Maryland vs. Chase Wyndham.

Court procedure in small Maryland county seats
brings tears to the eyes of young lawyers from Baltimore who know how things ought to be done. It can,
I think, be explained on the grounds that county
crime is normally confined to colored boys who
smash their grandmothers over the head with an ax
to get their savings, or to the domestic troubles of
their elders, or to transient whites who break in a
country store after hours. Justice takes on a personal quality that it can't have in large cities.

Judge Garth has sat behind the high raised plat-
form with the two old-fashioned lamps on either
end for thirty-two years. I've often been there as a
witness, and I imagine that the place is just about
as it was thirty-two years ago, except that the judge
is older. I sometimes look at his thin blue lips and
stern cold gray eyes and try to think what the
accumulated experience of all those years must have
done to him. I wondered, sitting there with Nat,
whether it makes a crime like the one Chase was being tried for, seem a terrible thing, to be severely
punished, or whether all the distress and crime that
he's seen has been transmuted in some way into a
deep understanding of the motives and desires that
move men.

Chase had come in, and was sitting with his attorney, de Forrest Blaine, a capable young man
from Baltimore. He was as immaculately clad and

brushed as ever, but on his face there was an expression of assumed confidence that looked very much like a thin maple veneer over gumwood. It always seems odd to me that handsome immaculate men like Chase and Richard Wyndham manage to look seedy and haggard much more quickly than rather unkempt homely people like Nat.

I glanced from Chase to Judge Garth seated above him. The contrast between their faces was so tremendous that it was almost a shock. I've tried to explain to myself what there was in Judge Garth's face that was so different from other men's. Looking at the two of them now, I thought I could tell. Chase's face was a sort of battleground of unfulfilled desire and emotion, discontent and indecision. Judge Garth had come to the end of desire. Discipline, I suppose it is. A soul completely and perfectly controlled.

Neither of the two, however, was as splendid and imposing as my friend Lieutenant Kelly, who was leaning against the rail in front of the jury box, talking to Mr. Taylor. He was sheer perfection. He had his pearl gray hat with the black band pushed on the back of his curly gray hair, which was carefully restrained with something that looked like Madame Arcola's best perfumed monkey-grease hair-straightener that Estaphine affects. When he came over, very like the host of the inn, to greet me, I found it smelled like it too. He had on a pink shirt and his brown suit with fine gray stripes. The

collar of his shirt was pinker than the main shirt.
I imagine he has two collars to that set. His necktie
was a light tan and green checkerboard effect. He
had a professional shave and his usual cigar. It may
have been my imagination, but I could have sworn
that the diamond in the ring on his little finger was
more lustrous than usual. There's no doubt, in any
case, that his smile was.

"It's all sewed up, Doc," he whispered to me,
coming back when he saw us. "Taylor's sure got a
break here, and boy, does he need it."

Then he added, I suppose in the way of making a
sporting proposition out of it, "But you can't tell
about them juries."

We shook hands solemnly. I don't know why—it
just seemed the thing to do. He went back to speak
to Mr. Taylor. Then he shook hands with Chase,
and with Chase's attorney. Mr. Taylor shook hands
with Chase and with a wide circle of people in the
front rows.

"Looks like a scene in a French café," Nat
grumbled to me. "Wish they'd quit shaking hands
and get at it."

They did in a moment. The clerk read out the
charge. Mr. Taylor looked about with the air of
leading character that he does so well, and at the
same time with a little the air of gladiator ready for
combat.

The first move of importance was a distinct surprise, and came from Chase's attorney. His client,

he announced, waived the right of trial by jury, and elected trial by the court. I suppose I should explain that Maryland law allows any person to choose what kind of a trial he will have. That is, whether he shall be tried by court or by jury. It's an interesting fact that a very large percentage of trials are by the court, especially in rural communities. But when Chase's lawyer made that announcement there was an audible gasp in the courtroom.

Lieutenant Kelly and Mr. Taylor looked sharply at each other. Lieutenant Kelly shook his head.

I felt my heart sink, and Nat said, "Jeez, that's just what everybody's been telling him not to do. Old Garth'd hang his grandmother."

Which certainly was one way of putting it. If Chase hoped for mercy from the gray, marble-faced, steely-eyed presence on the bench, he was a fool. With the facts that Taylor had against him, if Lieutenant Kelly could be believed, his only chance was a dramatic appeal to the jury. I had supposed that that was why he'd hired de Forrest Blaine, who was as much of an actor as he was attorney. Here he was pleading not guilty, and leaving his fate in the hand of a man who, however just, could not help but remember that he was trying the alleged poisoner of one of his oldest friends.

The trial began with the elaborate introduction of exhibits by the State's Attorney, running half way down the alphabet. There was the empty whiskey bottle found under the hedge at Stonehill, and

eighteen cigarette butts found in front of the porch.
There were photographs of finger-prints and plaster
casts of shoes. Most damning of all, there were two
small pellets found under the wall in the back garden of Wyndham House. Lastly Mr. Taylor introduced the bottle of pills that had been taken from
my bag at Mrs. Penniman's luncheon to Miss
Nettie.

Mr. Taylor's first witness was the state pathologist. He had examined the contents of Miss Antoinette Wyndham's stomach and had found one
of the glucosides of digitalis. He had examined the
contents of the dog's stomach, and found the presence of the same drug. He had examined the film
scraped from the surface of the mahogany bedside
table, and the residue in the water glass. He had
again found minute but definite quantities of digitalin. He had compared the drug found in the
bodies of Miss Wyndham and her dog and that on
the table and in the glass with that contained in the
two pellets found by Lieutenant Kelly in the back
garden, and found them identical. They in turn had
been compared with the pellets remaining in Mrs.
Penniman's bottle, and had been found identical.

Chase's attorney in cross examining asked how
much digitalin had been discovered. The pathologist regretted that he had no way of determining
the exact quantity.

"But it must have been a considerable amount,
to have done all the damage that's suggested."

The pathologist explained that his function was to determine the presence or absence of digitalis in the bodies of Miss Wyndham and her dog, on the table, and in the glass.

"Exactly," said Mr. Blaine. "I'm suggesting to you that there must have been a considerable amount present for you to do so. Is that correct?"

The pathologist agreed generally that it was.

"Would you say that digitalin is a rare or uncommon drug?"

"Not at all."

"It can be procured from any drug store?"

"Yes."

"Anyone suffering from heart disease would probably have the drug on hand?"

The pathologist maintained that that was out of his field, but agreed that it was probably true.

"So that in saying the drug found in Miss Wyndham's stomach and under a blade of grass in the back garden, is the same drug as that in the bottle spilled at Mrs. Penniman's luncheon does not say that it is not also the same drug that we could find in any drug store in the country, or in the medicine chest of any sufferer from heart disease."

"That's true."

"Thank you."

Mr. Taylor called me next.

I identified the bottle as the one taken from my bag, or similar to it, and testified that it doubtless was that from which I took the pill that quieted

Mrs. Penniman when she had her pseudoangina attack at the luncheon. I testified that seven pills were
unaccountably missing from the bottle. At Mr. Taylor's request I went into the nature of digitalin and
its effect on the heart.

"Now, Dr. Fisher. How many of these tiny pills
would be necessary to cause the death of an aged
person?"

"It depends entirely on the person," I replied.
"Very small doses of digitalin have been known to
cause death, and people have been known to recover
from very large doses."

"Then I'll put it this way, Dr. Fisher. Would five
of these tablets be sufficient to cause Miss Wyndham's death?"

"I think so, undoubtedly," I said.

"Thank you, Dr. Fisher."

Mr. de Forrest Blaine rose.

"Dr. Fisher," he said, "how large is the dose of
digitalin in one of these pills?"

"One one-hundredth of a grain."

"And you say that five of these tablets would kill
a woman seventy-five years old?"

"I believe so. Unless she were very robust."

"Would four one one-hundredth grain tablets kill
her?"

"Probably."

"Would three?"

"I shouldn't like to say so, definitely."

"There's a reasonable doubt in your mind?"

"Yes."

"Then, Dr. Fisher, if seven of these tablets were given to this old woman they would cause her death?"

"Yes."

"Now, would five one one-hundredth of a grain digitalin tablets be enough, Dr. Fisher, to cause Miss Wyndham's death, the death of her dog, and leave a substantial residue on the mahogany table and in the glass?"

"They might, possibly. I couldn't say any more than that."

"You won't be positive?"

"I shouldn't care to be."

"Thank you, Dr. Fisher."

I sat down. Nat Penniman was called and sworn.

He repeated in testimony the events of the luncheon that were now well known, probably, to everybody in the courtroom. He had brought my bag from the hall table and had taken the bottle of pills from it at my direction. He had been so frightened at his mother's attack that in the hurry to get the pills out for me he had spilled them on the floor. He had retrieved nine, which he had put on the table. He then paid no more attention to them until everyone except his father and I had left. He then had discovered that the nine pills were missing. Two were still left in the bottle.

"You looked around the floor then, Mr. Penniman?"

"Yes, and I found two more pills. But the other seven I'd picked up were gone."

"Now, Mr. Penniman. Did you see anyone near the table on which you had the pills?"

"No. I didn't notice anyone particularly."

"You didn't see the defendant standing near the table?"

"No. I didn't."

"Were you in the room the entire time, Mr. Penniman?"

"No, very little of it. I helped my father carry my mother upstairs to her bedroom."

"One more question, Mr. Penniman. You have recently married the defendant's cousin, have you not?"

Nat flushed.

"I have," he said.

One could see that this was one of Mr. Taylor's jury tricks, with very little point except to convey to a jury the impression that in some way they didn't quite understand Mr. Taylor had scored a small triumph. It obviously was not of much use with Judge Garth on the bench. Mr. Blaine rose smiling broadly.

"Congratulations, Mr. Penniman!" he said, and sat down. Mr. Taylor was visibly annoyed.

It was at the beginning of the second day of the Wyndham trial that Mr. Taylor called Richard Wyndham to the witness stand. The antagonism between Richard and his cousin was well known in town, and it was equally well known that Richard was the State's star witness. He got almost an ovation that morning when he parked his car in front of Mr. Lazenby's The Ladies Store and walked across the crowded square up the Court House steps. When Mr. Taylor called him he lounged up to the stand with as little concern as if he was going to a party in a parlor. It was perfectly obvious that he had the crowded courtroom with him to the last man —and woman. A discreet but distinct flurry of applause died instantly away at the sharp rap of Judge Garth's gavel and his stern forbidding frown.

Richard Wyndham, his customary half-cynical, half-amused smile on his full lips, and with his normal insolent bold stare, raised his right hand and swore to tell the truth, the whole truth and nothing but the truth, so help him God. Mr. Taylor, denied the jury that he'd relied on for his larger effects, recognized in his friendly audience a large and fairly important body of his supporters, and exhibited for their amusement the histrionics he usually reserved for the twelve good men and true in the box.

"Mr. Wyndham," he said, addressing his witness with an impressive courtesy that evidently didn't seem to his audience particularly inconsistent with the positively scurrilous attack he'd made on him at a political meeting in September, "where were you Tuesday, the day of your aunt's death, at one o'clock in the afternoon?"

"I went with my aunt to Mrs. Penniman's house for lunch."

"You saw the regrettable incident of Mrs. Penniman's collapse?"

"Yes."

"Did you see the pills Dr. Fisher called for spill out of the bottle and fall on the floor?"

"I did."

"Did you help to pick them up?"

"No."

"Where did you next see them, Mr. Wyndham?"

"On the table."

"Did you see anyone near the table later?"

"Yes," said Richard with great coolness.

"Tell the court who it was, and what you saw him do, Mr. Wyndham."

"I saw the defendant standing near the table, and sweep some object off it into his coat pocket."

"How far from him were you when you saw that?"

"About ten feet."

"Did you mention it to anyone?"

"No."

Mr. Taylor paused a moment to allow that its full effect, and proceeded.

"Now, Mr. Wyndham. Will you tell the court briefly what you did the rest of that day."

"I took my aunt home, and at her request called Dr. Fisher. She said she was ill. She certainly was wrought up. Dr. Fisher came, and my aunt then told me to call Judge Garth, which I did. When he came she sent me out of the room. I started downstairs when I heard a sound, which I'd sort of half heard, subconsciously, several times since I'd brought my aunt back from Mrs. Penniman's. At first I thought it was John, our colored man. I realized it wasn't and went downstairs to have a look about. I saw a couple of heel-marks on the cellar landing. Just then Dr. Fisher called me, and told me my aunt's pearls had been stolen."

"You then got the police, Mr. Wyndham—but leave that out and go on to the rest of your story of that afternoon."

"After Dr. Fisher, Judge Garth and the police had gone, I talked to my aunt a while, and finally persuaded her to go to bed. I telephoned Miss Daphne Lake after that, and asked her to stay at the house that night with my aunt."

"Why did you do that, Mr. Wyndham?"

"For two reasons. Miss Lake is the only woman my aunt liked, that I knew of, and I thought it would be good to have someone in the house. In the second place I wanted to watch Miss Lake."

"Why did you want to do that?"

"Because I was sure it was Miss Lake who was in the house that afternoon. I had begun to suspect Miss Lake of having a special interest in the house, and in view of the fact that my aunt's jewels were disappearing, and Miss Lake was the only outsider ever in the house, I was forced to put two and two

together. I thought I'd like to know what Miss Lake
was after that was important enough to make her
go into my aunt's house while we were away. I also
remembered that when my cousin Gail Wyndham
asked me to ask my aunt to go to Mrs. Penniman's
for lunch, I refused; and when I told Miss Lake,
she persuaded me to go. Well, when I saw the heel-
marks of a woman's shoe on the cellar landing, I
knew the noises had come from the cellar, and I
closed the doors and locked Miss Lake in. That was
just when Dr. Fisher was there. When I went back,
she was gone; she'd got out through the cellar window. I guessed she hadn't got what she wanted.
That's the chief reason I invited her back."

"What purpose did you expect that to serve, Mr.
Wyndham?"

Richard shrugged his shoulders.

"I figured I'd find out what she was after, and
maybe catch the fellow she was working with."

"Who was that?"

"I don't know. Some fellow I'd seen her with in a
car outside of town one day."

"All right, Mr. Wyndham. Tell the court what
you did next."

"I left the house when Miss Lake came, went to
the Greek's and got something to eat. About eight
o'clock I went back to the house, went around and
sat down in the grape arbor in the back garden."

"What did you expect to do there?"

"I expected to see whether anyone came to help

Miss Lake, and to see what she did. I did see her light through the chinks in one of the upstairs shutters. About nine o'clock I saw a light in the cartouche—that's the little window in the attic."

"What else, Mr. Wyndham?"

Mr. Taylor's manner so clearly indicated that this, after all, was the big moment, that I suppose nearly all of us leaned forward a little and listened even more intently. Richard went on as coolly and nonchalantly as before.

"About five minutes past nine," he said, "I saw my cousin Chase Wyndham, the defendant, come across the garden, and go into the house."

Mr. Taylor looked deliberately and impressively at him.

"How did you know, Mr. Wyndham," he said slowly, "that it was the defendant whom you saw there, in the garden, and entering the house, at about five minutes past nine o'clock?"

"He had a flashlight with him. I was sitting pretty close to the hyphen door. He went in that way. When he turned the light on the keyhole it showed his face up."

"All right, Mr. Wyndham. What did you see him do?"

"I saw him turn the lock and go in."

"Go ahead with your story, Mr. Wyndham."

"He was inside about ten minutes, then he came out at the same door."

"Did you notice anything unusual about the way he came out?"

"Yes. He was in a hurry. He seemed quite agitated. I assumed that he'd heard Miss Lake and was frightened. He has never been very courageous."

"Object, your honor," snapped Mr. Blaine, who had been listening with a sort of impatient suavity. His manner was in the most marked contrast with his client's, who had been leaning forward, pale and visibly disturbed. I wondered if it was possible that he hadn't known he'd been seen—if Richard Wyndham's story was true.

"Sustained," said Judge Garth. He was as immobile and impersonal as a figure of stone. I thought once or twice that I saw his face quiver, as if a sharp pain had gone through his body or soul; but looking at him again I decided that it was a trick of the light, and the flapping window shade over the empty jury box.

Mr. Taylor bowed.

"Now, Mr. Wyndham," he said, "did you see anything else unusual in the garden."

"Not at that time."

"Later?"

"Yes."

"At what time?"

"At about half after eleven."

"Tell the court what you saw."

"I saw the defendant come back again."

"Was he alone?"

"I didn't see anyone else with him."

"What did he do?"

"He went into the house again."

"How long did he stay?"

"I should say he came out in about three minutes."

"Did you notice anything peculiar about him?"

"I thought he was tight. He couldn't walk straight."

"Was that before or after he was in the house?"

"Before. He seemed steadier when he came out."

"Now, Mr. Wyndham, correct me if I'm wrong. I want this made perfectly clear. You saw the defendant, who is your cousin, Mr. Chase Wyndham, come into the garden of Miss Wyndham's house, on the night of her death, at nine o'clock, or at about nine o'clock. Is that right?"

"Yes."

"He went into the house, and came out again in about ten minutes."

"Yes."

"He came again at about half-past eleven, and stayed in the house about three minutes?"

"Yes."

"And the second time he came you believed that he was under the influence of liquor?"

"Yes."

"So that it would not surprise you if you knew that the defendant, the first time he went into the house, had killed . . ."

De Forrest Blaine sprang to his feet with an inarticulate shout.

"I object, your honor," he cried. "What would or would not surprise the witness——"

"Sustained," said Judge Garth coldly.

Mr. Taylor bowed again.

"That is all, Mr. Wyndham. Thank you."

Mr. Taylor smiled slyly and winked at someone in the front row as he resumed his seat.

Mr. Blaine rose.

"Mr. Wyndham," he said politely, "where were you at three o'clock on the afternoon of your aunt's death, after the luncheon at Mrs. Penniman's?"

"In Wyndham House with my aunt."

"And where were you at five o'clock that afternoon, Mr. Wyndham?"

"In Wyndham House."

"Now, Mr. Wyndham. I understood you to say that your aunt sent you out of the room to air her charming little pet, when Judge Garth had arrived, and that when you went into the hyphen you saw the prints of two heels on the cellar landing. Is that right?"

"Yes."

"Why didn't you investigate at once—or did you?"

"I didn't, because Dr. Fisher came and told me the pearls had been stolen."

"I see. Now, Mr. Wyndham. We have heard, from Dr. Fisher, how your aunt talked to her and

Judge Garth, how your aunt had Judge Garth read the will, and how she then discovered that the pearls were missing; and how Dr. Fisher then went downstairs for you. Now, Mr. Wyndham, I would like you to tell the court what you were doing all that time."

A slow flush spread over Richard's dark face.

"I was looking out the window," he said insolently.

"I suggest, Mr. Wyndham, that you were listening at your aunt's keyhole to see if she intended changing her will."

Richard half rose out of the witness chair, his jaw set in angry white ridges.

"I also suggest," Mr. Blaine went on calmly, "that that five minutes, or eight perhaps, before you went downstairs, was an excellent time to put some pills very much like the ones you think you saw the defendant take at Mrs. Penniman's in a glass——"

"Object, your honor," shouted Mr. Taylor, his face suddenly as red as a peony. "The witness is not on trial for this crime."

"Objection sustained," said Judge Garth.

Mr. Blaine nodded indifferently.

"Mr. Wyndham, did you invite Miss Lake to stay at your aunt's home that night, or did your aunt?"

"I did."

"Why?"

"I've already explained my reason. I was convinced that Miss Lake was a thief. I wanted to watch her."

"You're quite sure you weren't giving her an excellent chance to take anything you didn't want around?"

Richard made an obvious effort to control his very combustible temper.

"Quite," he said. "As far as I understand the question."

"Now, Mr. Wyndham. Did you take Miss Lake to see your aunt when she came?"

"No. My aunt didn't know she was in the house."

"I see," said Mr. Blaine meditatively. "In that case you were the last person to see your aunt alive."

"That I couldn't say," said Richard coolly.

Mr. Blaine moved closer to the witness stand, and fixed a contemptuous eye on Miss Nettie's favorite nephew.

"I suggest to you that Miss Wyndham was not alive when you saw her before Miss Lake arrived. I suggest that you admitted Miss Lake, knowing your aunt was dead."

"That's a lie."

"I suggest, Mr. Wyndham, that you sat in the garden, knowing your aunt was dead, waiting for someone to give the alarm. Miss Lake, probably."

"That is not true," said Richard equably.

Mr. Blaine's eyebrows rose.

"What did you do, Mr. Wyndham, after you saw the defendant leave the house?"

Richard hesitated slightly.

"I went into the house. I intended to speak to Miss Lake, but I didn't. I saw her go into the dining room and light a lamp there. Then she began to go through the highboy where my aunt kept the linen. She even spotted the secret drawer at the top. There's no doubt she knew her stuff. I decided then that she was hunting for something special. I slipped back of a bookcase in the hall and waited for her. She came out in a minute and went upstairs. I started up and must have made a noise, because she came down quickly. In a few minutes I heard her telephone, and I went down in the cellar to wait. Then in a few minutes I heard her let someone in the front door. It turned out to be Dr. Fisher."

"I suggest, Mr. Wyndham," said Blaine, "that you knew your aunt was dead when Miss Lake went upstairs, and that that is why you did not speak to her. You wanted her to find the body of your aunt."

"No," said Richard calmly. "I didn't know she was dead until Miss Lake told me so in front of Dr. Fisher when I came to the house later on, after I'd gone home."

"Now, Mr. Wyndham. Did you at any time open your aunt's desk?"

"Yes. As soon as Dr. Fisher had left and I was alone in the house, I went upstairs to get the will."

"Was the door of your aunt's room open?"

"No, it was locked. I unlocked it with the key to another door."

"Why did you do that, Mr. Wyndham?"

"In view of the fact that my cousin and Miss Lake had been in the house, I thought the will would be safest if I had it."

"Now, Mr. Wyndham, what time did you say your aunt went to bed?"

"At six forty-five."

"Did you help her?"

"Yes. I brought her supper and the dog's supper up on a tray, and I helped her get in bed. I sat there while she ate her supper, and said good night to her."

"Did you bring her a glass of water?"

"No."

"Did you put a number of small white pills in the water that she already had on her table?"

Richard smiled.

"No," he said coolly.

"You had opened your aunt's desk many times in your life?"

"Yes."

"Thank you. That's all."

In some way Richard Wyndham left the stand with his fine coat of nonchalance the least bit frayed. Mr. Blaine's questions and insinuations seemed only too pointless to me, but I could sense from the courtroom audience that they had somehow succeeded a little at least in tarnishing the

Richard Wyndham glamor. The undercurrent of approbation had nearly disappeared. I saw a number of people—including old Mr. Nelson Jacob—shake their heads as much as to say it was in no way a surprise to them, it was what they'd thought all along.

"Lieutenant Joseph Kelly!" said the clerk, and my resplendent friend took his place on the stand.

"Now, Lieutenant Kelly," said Mr. Taylor, "just tell the court about your activities in connection with this case."

It seemed that Lieutenant Kelly had faithfully kept me informed of his activities. He chiefly brought out the facts that he had pointed out to me in the garden. The State's exhibits were brought forward impressively, and I could see how the court-room was impressed. The plaster cast of the footprints beneath the wall Mr. Blaine, after examination, admitted to correspond exactly with the prints of his client. The pellets were admitted as undoubtedly of the same sort as those contained in my bottle. His unerring tracing of my own exploits Lieutenant Kelly did not mention.

"Now, Lieutenant Kelly," said Mr. Taylor, "I have here exhibit C, which I believe is a picture of the finger-prints found on the slant top of the secretary in Miss Wyndham's room."

"That's right."

"Where was this photograph taken?"

"In the bedroom where Miss Wyndham died."

"The room in which the body was found?"

"Yes, sir."

"That's all, Lieutenant. Call Sergeant Maxon."

Sergeant Maxon turned out to be of the Baltimore Police department of finger-prints, and he turned out to be armed with an enlarged chart of the prints, which after some trouble was admitted authentic.

"Sergeant, just explain the prints on this enlargement to the court."

The chart presented a curious and intricate pattern, to which Sergeant Maxon, a weazened little man, addressed himself with a pointer.

"There are prints of three different people here," he said, "overlapping. This print, which you can see part of here, belongs to Judge Garth. This one over it, which you can see part of to the right, here, corresponds to the prints of the defendant. Overlapping the two of these, now, but showing part of itself alone right here, to the bottom, is a third print, and it's identical with that of Mr. Richard Wyndham. It's a very unusual case," he added with a burst of professional interest, "but it happens once in a while."

"So that each of those hands touched that desk at successive times."

"Yes, sir."

"So we can assume with absolute certainty," continued Mr. Taylor, "that between the time Judge Garth opened the desk to give Miss Wyndham her will, and the time Mr. Richard Wyndham opened it, the defendant had undoubtedly touched that desk."

"Yes, sir."

"Have you any way of stating what time—knowing when Judge Garth and Mr. Richard Wyndham touched the desk—the defendant did so?"

"No, sir. Just that it was after Judge Garth and before Mr. Wyndham."

"That's all, Sergeant. Call Mr. Albert Thornton."

Mr. Thornton, whose new sons Lieutenant Kelly and I had visited, took the stand with some uneasiness.

"What is your occupation?" Mr. Taylor began amiably.

"I'm a farmer, as everybody knows."

I don't doubt that was a challenge to those people who have at times hinted that Mr. Thornton also ran a still.

"Where is your farm, Mr. Thornton?"

Mr. Thornton, instinctively suspecting this formality, eyed the State's Attorney uneasily.

"On the Lake road, ten minutes out from this here Court House."

"What were you doing, Mr. Thornton, on Tuesday night of Miss Wyndham's death, at half after ten o'clock?"

"Sittin' on my front porch."

"What did you see at that time?"

"I saw a car go by about seventy miles an hour."

"What kind of a car was it?"

"It was a long black sport car with a New York license."

"Which way was it going?"

"Towards the town."

One point in Mr. Blaine's cross examination surprised me, but I suppose such things naturally get out.

"What were you doing on the porch, now, Mr. Thornton?"

"Just studyin'."

"What were you studying?"

"Studyin'—thinkin' about things."

"Well, how could you tell it was a New York license?"

"There's a light in front of my place, and it's right on the road. I saw it."

"Mr. Thornton, how much money did Lieutenant Kelly give you the day you told him about seeing that car?"

"Ten dollars," said Mr. Thornton in great surprise. "He gave it to me for my twin boys."

"Ten dollars, eh? And you're sure it was half after ten."

"Yes, *sir.*"

Mr. Taylor's next witness was a familiar figure about town.

"Call Mr. James Digges," he said. "Your name?"

"Jimmy Digges, sir."

"Occupation?"

"I run the camera at the Gaiety. It's a movie."

The audience's titter stopped abruptly at Judge Garth's frown.

"What time do you get through work, Mr. Digges?"

"The last show's out at eleven, but I don't get away before twenty-five after."

"At what time did you leave the theater on the Tuesday of Miss Wyndham's death?"

"That time. Same time."

"Tell the court what you saw on the way home."

"I saw a girl running down Chase Street. She turned into the alley—I mean Fleet Street—and I wondered if something was the matter, so I followed her."

"Who was that girl, Mr. Digges? Did you recognize her?"

"Yes, sir. It was Miss Wyndham."

"Miss Gail Wyndham? The defendant's cousin?"

"Yes, sir."

"What did you see then?"

"I saw her get in a big black roadster parked down near Front Street."

"Was anybody in the car?"

"Yes, sir. Two men."

"Do you see either of those men in this court?"

"I wouldn't recognize 'em, sir. I thought I was

just buttin' into something, and there didn't seem to be any trouble, so I went back to Chase Street."

Mr. Blaine waived cross-examination with a smile. Mr. Taylor bent down and talked in an undertone to Lieutenant Kelly for a moment, then turned to the papers in front of him.

Then he straightened up and said, "Call Miss Daphne Lake."

There was a tense silence in the courtroom, while everyone waited, no one, I suppose, sure of what to think. Then I heard the sharp click of little heels as the girl came smartly down the aisle. I glanced around. She saw me and smiled, and I smiled back.

A little gasp went up when she went through the gate that the bailiff held open for her, and everyone got a full view of the little hairdresser's trim figure. She wore a light ermine coat and a tight-fitting little brown hat. She took the witness stand with the ease of a veteran and pulled off her hat without being told to do it. There she sat, with the same shining hair; but her face had changed. All the layers of make-up were gone. The long lashes over her brown eyes were no longer heavy with mascara. She was lovely to look at. The women in the courtroom stirred uneasily.

"Your name, please?"

"Daphne Lake."

"Your occupation?"

Daphne Lake smiled at me across the sea of gap-

ing faces whose heads—or whose wives' heads—she
had washed and waved.

"Private investigator for the Occidental Insurance Company," she said quietly.

CHAPTER

17

DAPHNE LAKE'S explanation of her activities was simple enough, as it turned out, but it nearly caused a riot in the courtroom. De Forrest Blaine objected time and again to its admission as evidence, and Judge Garth overruled him time and again. I don't know that it was so much on the strictest grounds of legal procedure as that it was obviously the only way that it could ever be accurately known what had happened behind those shuttered windows of Wyndham House.

And in one sense the facts that she told in her clear matter-of-fact voice were entirely to Chase Wyndham's advantage. It all depended on how they were interpreted. There certainly was nothing in them to add to the picture formed by Lieutenant Kelly and Mr. Taylor of his criminal guilt.

Considerably condensed, her story was this. The Occidental Insurance Company had insured Wyndham House and its contents under a Fine Arts policy for $150,000.

"This policy is what we call an All Risk Policy,

244

and carries protection against fire, theft and mysterious disappearance."

"Who arranged for the insurance with your company, Miss Lake?"

"Mr. Chase Wyndham."

"Who paid the premiums?"

"Mr. Chase Wyndham."

"Thank you. Go on, please."

"We also insured Miss Wyndham's jewelry under a so-called Jewelry Floater Policy. The actual intrinsic value of the gems was not large, but their extrinsic value, on account of their age, workmanship and so on, was fairly large. They were insured, altogether, for $10,000."

"Who paid the premium for that policy?"

"Mr. Chase Wyndham. My company accepted this insurance with some reluctance, because the house was not protected adequately, either from theft or fire. However, there had never been a recorded theft of any article from Wyndham House. Then, while the house wasn't wired for electricity, there was a constant danger from oil lamps and open fires. Still, the local fire departments are superior organizations, and we accepted the risk. I may also add that the artistic prominence of the house makes it a publicity asset, even considering the responsibility involved.

"The policy had been in effect only three months when Miss Wyndham reported the theft of a pair of paste shoe buckles valued at $150.00. Normally

no investigation would have been made, but in view
of the peculiar situation and the value of the other
contents of the house, we sent a man down. He
reported it a case of mysterious disappearance, and
we paid the $150.00."

"To whom, Miss Lake?"

"To Miss Wyndham."

"Continue, please."

"One month later we received notice that a Queen
Anne coffee pot valued at $1,200 had disappeared.
We then began a financial investigation of Miss
Wyndham, and found that she was financially
sound. But it seemed that something was wrong
somewhere. I was then sent down with another investigator. He had made a preliminary inspection,
had found nothing out of the way but thought the
whole affair looked rather queer. I then took a position at Miss Chew's beauty shop and watched Miss
Wyndham and Wyndham House. My company has
a large sum involved, and if there was any suspicion about the sanity or good will of the insured,
we would at once cancel the policy. Normally that
is what would have been done at that point."

"Why wasn't that done in this case, Miss Lake?"

"Because we had nothing to go on except hearsay
that Miss Wyndham and the old Negro servant
were mad. Then we could also be legally involved
if we made a false step. But it was chiefly because
of the artistic prominence of the house. Then it

would look odd, and insurance companies don't like things to look odd—ever."

"So you set yourself to watch the house and its owner. Did you discover anything unusual?"

"Yes."

"Tell the court about it, Miss Lake."

"I found out at once that the Wyndhams were not on friendly terms. That three of her brothers' children never visited Miss Wyndham. That Richard Wyndham was his aunt's favorite and was in and out of the house constantly. I got to know Richard Wyndham quite well. He always had a good deal of money, but I couldn't find out where he got it. Mr. Wyndham was extremely reticent on any subject involving his own affairs. Meanwhile, a number of other objects disappeared, and we paid claims amounting to around $4,000. Still we had no grounds for taking action. It could have been a sneak thief of an unusual kind. We have had many antiques stolen by apparently very respectable people."

"Now, Miss Lake, you say you kept a close watch on Wyndham House."

"I and the other investigator together."

"Did you ever see the defendant at the house?"

"Yes. About three weeks before Miss Wyndham's death I got into the garden at ten o'clock at night. I saw a man there who went into the house through the hyphen door. I followed him upstairs and heard him speak to Miss Wyndham. She was in bed. He woke her up, and they talked about half an hour."

"Did you hear him threaten her unless she gave him money?"

"I object, your honor!"

"Overruled," said Judge Garth.

"Yes."

"Who was that man?"

"It was the defendant."

"How do you know it was the defendant?"

"I left the house first and got over the wall. I saw a car there, with a New York license, and thought it was my associate's. He sometimes parked in Front Street when I was in the garden. I got in it, and was surprised when Mr. Chase Wyndham—the defendant—jumped over the wall and got in the car. He was surprised too."

"What did you do, Miss Lake, then?"

Daphne Lake smiled.

"We went to the Blue Moon on the Mountain Road and had soft crabs and beer."

"Did the defendant tell you anything that evening that made you suspect his aunt was in any danger from him?"

"Nothing."

"Was the evening entirely wasted, Miss Lake?"

"Not at all. I learned that the defendant thought Mr. Richard Wyndham was getting away with articles on which the defendant was paying the insurance."

"Did he express the fear that someone might burn the house down?"

"He did."

"What did you do about that?"

"I got in touch with my associate, and together we kept an almost constant watch on the house. I didn't feel that it was really in danger unless something happened to annoy Miss Wyndham extremely."

"You say you got to know Mr. Richard Wyndham?"

"Very well."

"Did you ever at any time feel that the house was in any danger from him?"

"Never."

"Now, Miss Lake. Where were you Tuesday, when Miss Wyndham was at Mrs. Penniman's for lunch?"

"I was in Wyndham House."

"For what purpose?"

"I was then convinced that the stolen articles had never left the house. I wanted to make a search while no one else was in the house."

"What did you find?"

"Nothing. Miss Wyndham and Mr. Richard Wyndham returned before I was through one room. I got out through the hyphen into the garden, but had to go back because old John was in the grape arbor, smoking a pipe. I didn't want him to see me."

"You were in the house again that day?"

"Yes."

"When was that?"

"At night. When Miss Wyndham came in with Mr. Richard Wyndham she was extremely upset. Her voice was trembling and she kept rapping her stick on the floor. I heard her say that she would burn down the house before Mrs. Penniman should ever get it. And she said she meant what she said."

"You heard her say that yourself?"

"Yes."

"What time was it when you returned that night?"

"About seven o'clock."

"Where were you at nine o'clock, Miss Lake?"

"At nine I was upstairs."

"Did you raise a window?"

"Yes."

"What for?"

"I was signaling to my associate. I'd phoned him to keep an eye on the garden while I was inside."

"Did you hear anything in the house that night?"

"Yes. I heard someone around nine o'clock moving around in Miss Wyndham's room. I thought it was Miss Wyndham herself at first. I couldn't hear very distinctly. I was in the attic at the time, and had closed the trap-door in case anyone came in."

"Do you still think it was Miss Wyndham?"

"No."

"Why not?"

"Because I heard whoever it was leave very hurriedly."

"Did you think it was Mr. Richard Wyndham?"

"No."

"Why not, Miss Lake?"

"Because I know Mr. Wyndham's step very well."

"Didn't you investigate?"

"Yes. As soon as I could get down out of the attic I did. He had left by that time."

"How long was that person in Miss Wyndham's room?"

"I think about four or five minutes."

"Did you hear the sound of voices there, Miss Lake?"

"No. I couldn't, of course, even if they were talking, unless they shouted. The walls are two feet thick."

"Now, Miss Lake. I want you to think what you were doing at half after eleven o'clock that night."

"At half past eleven I was just starting for the cellar."

"You were stopped by something?"

"Yes. As I came down the stairs I saw someone open the door from the hyphen and come into the lower hall."

"Did you see who it was?"

"Yes. It was the defendant."

"How could you recognize him, Miss Lake? The hall was unlighted, of course?"

"Yes. He had lighted his cigarette lighter and was staring about. The light showed his face quite clearly."

"Was there anything strange about him?"

"Yes. He was terribly excited. I wasn't very far from him. I could smell a strong odor of whiskey."

"What did he do?"

"I'm afraid I made a noise on the stairs. He turned and ran back into the hyphen and outside."

"He didn't at that time, then, go near Miss Wyndham's room?"

"No."

"Well, Miss Lake, what did you do then?"

"I sat on the stairs and waited until everything was quiet. I stayed there about fifteen minutes by my watch. My light was almost burned out, and I remembered that I'd seen a flashlight once in Miss Wyndham's room when I was combing her hair. I decided to see if it was there still. First I thought I'd try the oil lamp in the dining room. I lighted it and looked around in that room. But what I was looking for would probably be pretty well hidden, and with the oil lamp you couldn't see into corners at all.

"I went upstairs and went into Miss Wyndham's room. As I did so I heard a sound that came from way downstairs. I stood still and listened. I didn't hear anyone breathing in the room. My first thought was that Miss Wyndham was awake and had seen me, so I thought I'd just tell her what it was all about. I said, 'It's Daphne Lake, Miss Wyndham,' and I turned on my weak light. The minute I saw her I knew she was dead."

"Then what, Miss Lake?"

"Then I realized that this might be the only chance I'd have of looking in that room. I picked up her house gown that was lying on a chair and looked in the pockets."

"What for, Miss Lake?"

"Anything I could find. Then I saw something that showed me I was on the right track. There was a dusty cobweb clinging to the shoulders of it. I put the dress down and went out into the hall. I kept hearing that noise from the cellar. Then I sort of lost my nerve and called Dr. Fisher. She came in a minute or two. I didn't tell her I'd seen Miss Wyndham."

"Why not?"

"My job was to protect the house and find out what had happened to the lost articles. I'd come to the conclusion that the jewels were in the house. It was my belief that Miss Wyndham had stolen them herself and hid them, in order to collect the insurance. I thought that perhaps someone else had found where she'd hidden them, and I wanted to get them before they were really stolen. I thought the person in the cellar probably knew that Miss Wyndham was dead, and was trying to get them. So when Dr. Fisher came I did my best to get her down into the cellar first, but she insisted on looking to see if Miss

Wyndham was all right. When she saw what had happened she agreed with me that we should see who was in the house. I suppose she knew Miss Wyndham was murdered. She wouldn't give a certificate. Then when we went to the cellar, my chief idea was to frighten whoever was there away until I could have a look around myself."

"Did you see who it was?"

"Yes. It was Mr. Richard Wyndham. I saw him when he struck Dr. Fisher's arm. I pretended to faint then because I didn't want him to know I'd recognized him."

"Go on, please, Miss Lake."

"We then telephoned the coroner and Mr. Richard Wyndham. I'd purposely refrained from telephoning him until I knew he was home, because I didn't want him to be sure I knew what he was doing. Then when Mr. Wyndham came I went out."

"You were willing to leave him there in the house when you were so anxious before that he shouldn't be in the cellar?"

"Surely. Now that I knew it was Mr. Wyndham, and knew that he knew his aunt was dead, there'd hardly be any point in worrying about him. The place was his. He expected to inherit the house. I didn't then know the will was gone."

"Now, Miss Lake, you said before that you thought whoever was in the cellar knew Miss Wyndham was dead."

"I thought it was likely, since they were making

so much noise. But that was before I knew it was Richard Wyndham. I'm sure he didn't know his aunt was dead."

"Why, Miss Lake?"

"The way he acted when Dr. Fisher told him."

"What did he say?"

"I don't remember exactly. But it wasn't the sort of thing you'd say if you'd just murdered somebody."

"Thank you, Miss Lake."

Mr. Taylor sat down. Mr. Blaine rose with elaborate courtesy.

"Miss Lake," he said, "will you tell the court just what sort of thing Mr. Richard Wyndham said about his aunt?"

"He said he hated her. It was time she died. Something like that."

"You consider that the type of remark a man doesn't make if he has murdered someone?"

"Yes."

"Now, Miss Lake, you knew Mr. Richard Wyndham very well, did you not?"

"Yes."

"It was even rumored, I believe, that you were to marry him. Is that true?"

"It is not," said Daphne with a smile. "Mr. Wyndham made a good many proposals to me, but marriage was not one of them."

"Had him that time," said Nat, turning to me and grinning from ear to ear.

The next two days of the trial brought out a train of damning evidence against Chase Wyndham. Eliot was called to the witness stand. He was forced to admit that his brother had left him Tuesday night to talk with Gail. He came back in about half an hour and suggested the two of them go out to Stonehill. At Stonehill he had been greatly upset, smoked constantly and nervously, and drank pretty heavily. He had then told Eliot about his loan from Miss Nettie. Suddenly, just before half past ten, he had sprung up and said he had to see his aunt again that night.

Eliot had remonstrated with him, tried to persuade him; but it was useless. Finally, realizing that his brother was half-drunk and had all the inebriate's stubbornness, Eliot had gone with him to the car and they had come back to town. They came to Wyndham House. They knew, of course, that the gates were locked; but there was a place where the wall was easy to climb.

When they were there, Eliot again tried to persuade his brother to give up the idea of going in the house. As he was arguing with him their cousin Gail Wyndham ran up. She had seen their car and was afraid something had happened. Eliot explained the situation, and told her that Chase insisted on seeing their aunt that night. She also tried to persuade him to go home and see her in the morning. He said it would be too late. He got rather violent, his voice getting louder and louder, and at last they decided it was best to let him go. Both worried, they followed him over the wall, Eliot lifting Gail down. They saw no one in the garden. The defendant then ran rapidly if not very accurately up to the hyphen and went in. The two of them stayed by the wall. He came back in a very short time, probably less than five minutes, considerably sobered. He then said that someone was in the house, and that their aunt was dead.

They had then talked it over, and decided to tell the story about the two men's going to Stonehill and Gail's staying home all evening. They then took Gail home and went to their hotel, seeing me leaving my house just as they arrived at it.

And Gail's story was the same, except that it contained the explanation of her being on the streets at that time of night. She had wanted to talk to Nat Penniman after her cousins had gone. She telephoned to him, and he came down. They had sat out in my back garden and talked until nearly eleven o'clock, when Nat went home. Gail stayed out on the porch a few minutes, and saw her cousins drive by. She knew the state Chase was in, and guessed what they were going to do. She was particularly alarmed because she had a half-suspicion that Miss Wyndham really planned to burn down the house that night.

She ran after them and saw them turn into Fleet Street. The rest of her story agreed with Eliot's. She knew nothing about where the defendant had been in the half hour between a quarter to nine and a quarter past nine. She had thought the defendant looked pale, but had not attributed it to anything particular. She knew he had been having business worries.

Mr. Taylor summed up simply and logically, and with what I, and I suppose everyone else, took to be almost conclusive reasoning.

Mr. Chase Wyndham was in great financial distress. His note for $10,000, with interest at ten per cent, was due in one week. He had no prospects except bankruptcy. At luncheon at the Pennimans' he had picked up the seven pills that had been dropped from the floor, sweeping them off the table into his coat pocket. That night at nine o'clock he had taken them with him to his aunt's house, got over the wall, dropping two of the pellets as he did so, and had entered the house and gone upstairs to his aunt's room.

Silently in that house of terror he had put the pills into the glass of water at the sick table of this poor defenceless old woman, the blood sister of his dead father. He had then opened the desk and had stolen her will, which he knew left the entire property to his cousin Richard Wyndham. He had then come back to his brother and cousin with the blood of their common ancestor on his hands, and then, like the miserable dissipated creature that he was, he had taken his tobacco and his bootleg whiskey and gone, not to his hotel, not to a speakeasy, but

to the home of his parents, the home of his child-
hood. There, we had it from his own brother, who
had perjured himself to save him, he had drunk
himself into a state of intoxication, railing at the
same time against that helpless old lady, the last of
the old aristocracy of Maryland. Then, besotted and
wanting to make sure that his nefarious attempt had
been successful, he had returned. But he was afraid.
Afraid of the dark, of a noise on the stairs! but not
afraid to use the foul means of poison to save himself from disaster. Had he not dropped two of the
pills he had stolen when he jumped from the wall
around Wyndham House, the State might never
have brought him to the gallows.

On Friday Mr. Blaine opened his case for the
defense. He called five doctors who held that at
least ten one one-hundredth grain tablets of digitalin would have been necessary to kill Miss Wyn-
ham and her dog and leave the residue in the glass
and on the table, and that five tablets could never
have done it. He called me and Dr. Michaels to
prove that at twelve-fifteen when I saw her and at
twelve-thirty when he saw her she might have been
dead five hours or possibly more. The rest of his
defense he based on the testimony of Chase Wyndham.

The atmosphere in the courtroom that greeted
the defendant when he stepped up to the stand and
took the oath was very different from that which
had greeted his cousin Richard. People seemed to

resent the jaunty and immaculate gray suit he wore,
even though the face above it was pale and lined.
His eyes had deep circles under them and he kept
biting at his tiny black mustache with his lower
teeth. I could see that he was making a desperate
effort to appear controlled.

I think Mr. Blaine must have been glad that he
had no jury that had to be impressed with his
client's innocence.

"Now, Mr. Wyndham," he said, with a sympathetic and confidential tone in his mellow voice that
managed to give the impression of utter veracity
and sincerity, "I want you just to tell the court
simply and honestly what you did on the Tuesday
of Miss Wyndham's death. It's not necessary for
you to explain what your financial situation is. We
have heard that, and you admit it. It's not an uncommon one these days. Nor do you have to tell the
court that you had any affection for your aunt. We
know that none of her nephews or her niece had
any. We're not trying to impress this court with any
spurious bathos. We aren't trying to force pity for
you, or to express any for a dead woman who had
neither pity nor love when she was alive. All we
want is the truth. I want you, Mr. Wyndham,
merely to tell the court exactly what you did on
that Tuesday."

Judge Garth looked up suddenly at this astonishing speech. He looked intently at Chase Wyndham.
I saw again a little spasm of pain cross his iron

brows. The line between his eyes deepened, and his jaw seemed set a little more tightly. He had a pen in his hand and was slowly and painstakingly writing notes on the defense's plea.

"I went to Mrs. Penniman's home to that luncheon," Chase began. "My aunt was there and the situation was extremely unpleasant. When those pills fell on the floor I thought suddenly that there was a way out of my difficulties. I knew a man who'd committed suicide that way, by simply taking an overdose of a common medicine. So when Mr. Nathan Penniman put them on the table I picked them up and put them in my pocket, I thought without being seen. Richard Wyndham left with my aunt, and the two Pennimans and Dr. Fisher came downstairs. We talked a minute or two and my brother and I left.

"When I took those pills, I had no intention of giving them to anybody. I intended to take them myself. But the more I thought about it the more obvious it became that I could give them to my aunt instead of myself. I thought about it all afternoon. At dinner my cousin, my brother and I were still talking about the things our aunt had done to our family and all that sort of thing. I finally worked myself up to the point where it seemed that to do away with her was the only thing to do.

"I left Dr. Fisher's house, told my cousin and my brother I'd be back in a few minutes, and went to Wyndham House. I'm not saying I wasn't perfectly responsible for anything I did, but I was so worked up I hardly knew what I was about. I got over the back wall where we used to climb sometimes when we were kids. I guess that's when I dropped two of the pills.

"I went to the hyphen door. I opened it with the clapper on the bell that hangs there. The clapper unhooks and you can work the lock with it. We used to do that when we were children too. Then I went right up to my aunt's room. Nothing has been changed in the house, but I had a flashlight with me from my car anyway. I went up to her room and over to her bed. Everything was silent as the grave.

"Suddenly it occurred to me that I would talk to her again, and maybe she'd be more reasonable in the matter of her loan to me. I turned on my flash and saw her all lopped over. She was dead. I didn't see the dog.

"Then all of a sudden it struck me that it wouldn't do me any good. My cousin Richard would get all her money, and wouldn't give me an inch more leeway than my aunt would have done. I remembered where she kept the will. She got it out and read it to me the last time I saw her, three weeks before, when I borrowed the ten thousand from her.

"I thought, of course, that she'd died naturally. It seemed like a chance in a million. I took it, I didn't stop a minute to think about it. I opened the desk, but the will was gone. I thought she'd probably stowed it away somewhere in town, now that I was here. She'd often accused me of stealing her things. She did everybody, even her two or three old friends.

"Well, then I went downstairs to the cupboard in the hall under the steps and opened the door. There's a place in it where they used to keep papers and things, a sort of secret locker that looks like a pine panel. I opened it. I didn't see the will, though I thought I had at first. But I saw something else."

He stopped suddenly and wiped the streaming perspiration from his forehead. We leaned forward, waiting. Family loyalty is a strange thing. I think that in spite of everything Chase Wyndham actually hated to have to say what finally came from him in a strained lowered voice.

"What did you find there, Mr. Wyndham?" said his attorney gravely, letting his eyes wander over the crowded room. You could have heard a mouse run across the floor.

"I found an old-fashioned typewriter, a Royal, and a sheaf of letters. I thought they were the will at first. I opened one of them and read it. It was a letter to my cousin Gail Wyndham, badly typed and illiterate, saying—well, all sorts of perfectly foul things. I opened another. I won't say what they were, except one of them that I read. That was a letter with a list of six people in town to get copies of it, saying that a certain man in this town was spending his time and his depositors' money in Richmond with a woman, and that he was on the point of leaving. It was that letter, as I guess everybody knows, that started the run on his bank and ruined a good many people beside himself. Well, my aunt had written those letters."

The tense silence in the court snapped like a taut cable. Judge Garth, his jaw set like a trap, brought his gavel down on the bench.

"Go on, Mr. Wyndham," said the attorney.

"Then I heard someone moving upstairs. I put the letters in my pocket and got out as quick as I could. I'd forgot all about the will. All I remembered was that old woman upstairs and those foul letters in my pocket.

"I went back to Dr. Fisher's and put the rest of the pills down the washbowl. I was glad my aunt was dead. I was thankful that I didn't have her blood on my hands."

Chase bent his head a moment, drew a deep breath, and looked up.

"I wanted to get away from there. I suggested to my brother that we drive out to Stonehill. I took a drink. I guess it went to my head, because I took another and another. Then I finished the bottle. The more I drank the more I thought about all this. Then I got the idea of going back to get that typewriter out, and do away with it so nobody'd ever find it. I wasn't thinking about the will then. I didn't want my cousin Gail, or my brother—or everybody—to know about my aunt.

"You know the rest of it. I went back. I was tight. My cousin and my brother tried to get me not to go. They didn't know why I wanted to go, and I couldn't tell them. They came over the wall with me and waited. I went in the house. I wanted to get in that closet under the stairs. I'd dropped my flashlight somewhere, so I took out my cigarette lighter. It didn't give much light. Then I heard a noise close to me, in the dark. That sobered me up. I got out as fast as I could go. Gail and my brother got me over the wall. I told them the old woman was dead, but I didn't tell them anything else."

He wiped off his forehead again and drew a deep breath.

"That's the whole story," he said simply. "I didn't kill my aunt. I didn't take her will, or destroy it, or even touch it. The only thing I've destroyed is a pack of letters, which I previously showed to two people—my attorney, and my cousin Richard Wyndham. I burned those letters in their presence."

"Thank you, Mr. Wyndham," said his attorney. He turned to Mr. Taylor. Mr. Taylor hesitated a second, then shook his head.

"Your honor," said Mr. Blaine, "the case for the defense is closed."

A little sigh rippled through the room, and every eye turned to Judge Garth, sitting as passive and unmoved by Chase Wyndham's story as if he had been a marble statue. Yet while we watched him

his face seemed to turn a grayish-white under our
eyes. His jaw set in white ridges. He thrust back
his thin shoulders and sat erect; his left hand
reached forward and grasped the edge of the bench
rigidly, as though he were laboring under some great
emotion or pain. The courtroom waited in an almost
awed silence. Then suddenly his left arm was flung
out in a spasmodic gesture. His right hand pressed
against his heart, and his face was twisted with
agony.

"*Not guilty!*" he said quietly, and fell forward
on the bench.

I was the first person beside him, and I had already recognized that agonized convulsion of the
face and throat. Judge Garth was dead: angina pectoris—not Alice Penniman's false angina, but the
true. They cleared the courtroom, and we got him
into his private chamber. The white-haired bailiff
stood beside me wringing his hands.

"I've been with him thirty years," he said sadly.
"He's had this a long time."

It's odd how at such a moment slight things snap
up into your consciousness. I could see then, as
plainly as the day I actually saw it, Dr. Maxfield
Burton's great car turning up the road to the Pennimans'. And I'd thought Sam had called him in for
Alice. And then I remembered the times I'd wondered about the old judge's appearance, and had
recognized unconsciously, without ever actually
thinking it, those unmistakable symptoms. I thought

now of the first day of this whole affair, when I'd met him on my way up to the Pennimans', stopping to rest on his way up the hill, leaning against the telephone post for support.

The bailiff touched me on the arm.

"Excuse me, Doctor—I reckon he left this note for you. It's what he was writing on the bench. Got you-all's name on it."

He handed me a small sheet of paper with a brief line written on it.

It was the day after the bells of St. Margaret's had tolled their slow, sonorous accompaniment as the stern-lipped old man went down to his last long sleep under the tulip poplars by the river. I left my car parked in front of the closed gates of Wyndham House and crossed the street. The blinds in the Garth house were still drawn. I went up the steps and lifted the knocker. I had hardly let it fall when old Joseph opened the door. He must have been waiting there.

"It's a pleasure to see you-all, Doctah," he said. I thought for a moment he had got himself mixed up with his dead master, who always had said that. Before I could say anything he went on, "The jedge done lef' a paper fo' yo' under his blotter, Doctah. Ah been afraid somebody'd git it, so I done kep' it heah."

He pulled a folded piece of foolscap out of his

pocket and handed it to me. It was sealed with red wax and stamped with the arms of the Garths.

"Thank you, Joseph," I said.

"You'll like to go in the jedge's liberry, Miss?"

The judge's chair was there as it had always been. The musty smell of old books and old tobacco still hung about it. The turkey carpet with green swirls was worn in spots. I sat down in the horsehair armchair and waited for Joseph to go.

He eyed me with native indecision. He put his hand on the back of Judge Garth's empty chair and caressed it tenderly.

"The jedge done tol' me twenty yeahs ago, Doctah," he said at last, gravely, "that if yo' had a secret to keep, yo' certainly should keep it to yo'-self."

"That's true, Joseph," I said.

He nodded his head wisely.

"Yas *ma'am*. Ah jus' thought that was a very good thing to know about."

He bowed solemnly and left the room, closing the door very quietly.

I broke the seal on the paper that Judge Garth had addressed to me in his firm spidery hand. It was the document that the last note he'd written, while Chase Wyndham was on the stand, had directed me to find, read, and use at my discretion.

"Dear Madam," it read. "Since my talk with you I have seen my physician, Dr. Burton, who advises me that I will not survive another attack of angina, for which he has treated me for a number of years. He tells me that I must avoid nervous strain and emotional excitement; and as the present situation makes it impossible for me to do so without shirking my duty, I am now leaving this statement, in order that no innocent person shall suffer in the event of my death before the Wyndham case is disposed of. I leave it to your discretion to use in whatever way you think is proper.

"I administered the poison that caused the death of Antoinette Wyndham.

"I have long regarded that act as my duty. I have not sentenced a murderer to the gallows in the last ten years that I have not felt that a more dangerous criminal remained at large, living in luxury at Wyndham House, free.

"After the run on Henry Watts's bank, one of the letters that started it was brought to me. It happened that I recognized the machine that had written it at once. It was written on an old Royal typewriter that I had myself given to Eliot Wyndham when he was a boy. One of my nephews had broken off the 'n' key, and I had never had it repaired. I at once accused Antoinette Wyndham of writing the letter. She denied it; but no more letters were written for a number of years.

"Some years ago, they began again. I heard only rumors of them until Gail Wyndham brought me a letter that only her aunt could have written. After that I watched her; and twice, when she had gone out at dusk to the post-box, Gail Wyndham brought me letters that she had received the following day. I advised her to burn them without opening them. I believe she did that. I think she finally suspected her aunt, although I never told her.

"I have regarded Antoinette Wyndham's death as a necessary thing for many years. I have thought often of the good that her death, and the destruction of her unjust will would do. I have attached no more personal moral responsibility to my act in causing her death than I attach to passing a death sentence on a murderer, or to the hangman's act in executing that sentence.

"I had never thought exactly how I should do away with her until that day at the Pennimans' luncheon. When the tablets of digitalin fell to the floor, Antoinette Wyndham leaned over to me and whispered, 'That's foxglove—that's what old John killed his wife with.' At that time I did not know that any of the pills had disappeared.

"That afternoon I was preparing to go to Wyndham House when Richard telephoned saying his aunt wanted me to come at once. I dissolved ten pellets of digitalin, which Dr. Burton prescribed for me in case of a sudden attack, in a small bottle of water, and put it in my pocket. I went to Wyndham House. I realized when Antoinette Wyndham began to talk about giving her pearls to Gail that something was on foot again to discredit the girl. I did not know then, as Mr. Taylor told me later, that Miss Lake had discovered that presumably Antoinette was stealing her own jewels in order to collect their insurance. When I read her will that day, I saw to my surprise that it had not been properly witnessed. While you, Dr. Fisher, were out of the room, I explained that to Antoinette. She said she had never had it witnessed, because if her nephew Richard knew that he was sure of getting the property he would kill her without a qualm. She then said she would draw a new will and have it properly witnessed, and also told me that she couldn't bear actually to give her things away, because if she did she would die, and she was afraid of death.

"She then asked me to bring her water from the bathroom next to her room. I took her glass and emptied the contents of my bottle in it and filled it with water. I took it back to Anoinette. She barely sipped it and put it down on the table.

"She then asked me to take her will home with me and have it made out again and returned to her for signature. She lay down on her bed again. She laughed. I asked her what she was amused at. She replied that it had taken her seventy-five years to learn the value of a 'moral' man—I was the only person living of whom she had no fear. She said she had her dog eat half her food before she touched it. She knew John had tried to kill her a dozen times, and that Richard would do so also as soon as he knew her will was properly executed.

"Later, when I offered casually to get her fresh water, she winked at me.

"I left the house and went home. At first I thought I would keep the will, which was invalid; but I was not sure that I would survive even two days, or two hours. I thought that if the will should happen to fall into Richard's hands it would be a plain temptation to forge the signatures of dead servants, and that such a plan might succeed. I kept the will two days. I burned it the night that you, Mr. Taylor and Lieutenant Kelly were in my study.

"In saying that I have no feeling of personal moral responsibility in this matter, I have to make a further confession.

"I believe that there is a higher power that guides the justice of men. I believe that if I had no personal desire to see Antoinette Wyndham suffer, the train of circumstance that led to the discovery that she was murdered would never have been set up, and I should never have had to write this to you. The accident of the pills at Mrs. Penniman's; the accident of Miss Lake's being in the house that night and calling you; the accident of the dog's lapping up the water spilled from the glass when Antoinette was suddenly seized and knocked it over: those things would not have happened had I not been as truly guilty of murder as any other man who deliberately takes the life of another human being.

"In my soul I know now that I killed Antoinette

Wyndham not from any abstract ideal of justice. I killed her because I hated her with a deep and lasting hatred. Thirty-five years ago I loved Gail Seaton. We were to be married. One morning I got a letter saying things about her that were terrible and unbelievable. I learned later that she also got a letter, about me. As such things happen, we met, and each looked at the other, not believing, yet believing and silent. She married Gail Wyndham's father, I never married. Then Antoinette, whom I could never love, told me that she had done that thing. Years have passed, and she has never ceased tormenting me. Since Gail has grown, the picture of her mother to me, I have lived in constant fear of what that old woman would do to her.

"When I left Wyndham House, I left with a great weight lifted from my soul. But now I do not find it easy to take any punishment but the death which I know is waiting for me at each corner of the road, behind each door I enter, beside every chair I occupy. This is my statement. I do not wish anyone else to suffer for my act.

"Thos. R. Garth."

I folded the long closely-written sheet of foolscap, and stared into the empty fireplace a long time. I didn't hear the door open or anyone come in. I took a paper folder of matches out of my bag and knelt down on the old black bearskin in front of the fireplace. I struck the match and held it to the edge of Judge Garth's last statement of the force that had ruled his life. I watched the bright flame climb up, until I dropped the paper, a sheet of flame, into the grate. I watched it curl into a black-ened sheet, and I took the poker and broke the sheet into irrevocable and silent dust.

I got to my feet and turned around. In front of the closed door stood Lieutenant Kelly, freshly brushed and shaved, his diamond solitaire gleaming cheerfully from his little finger on the hand holding his very light gray hat with the black band.

Neither of us said anything for a while.

Then I said, "Well?"

And he said, "Well, well!" with a queer smile.

"So he *did* do it," he added then, gravely.

I said nothing.

"I thought he did, all along," said Lieutenant Kelly.

"No!" I protested ironically.

He flushed a little.

"Well, now," he said, "I did as soon's I seen you coming here. What'd he say in that?"

He nodded at the fireplace.

"Do you know, Lieutenant," I said, "somebody told me something a few minutes ago that I think is very true."

"Yeah?" he said uneasily. "What's that, now?"

"If you have a secret to keep, you certainly ought to keep it to yourself."

He smiled.

"Okay, Doc," he said cheerfully. "Now I'll tell you one, just to show there's no hard feeling."

"Yes?"

"You know who I thought bumped the old girl off and pocketed the will?"

"Chase Wyndham," I said. "Obviously."

"That was Taylor," he said easily. "I knew he never done it. That was just a gag. Nope, it wasn't him."

"Eliot?"

"No, but he could of. He was there, and he had as much reason as any of 'em. I thought there was something phoney about him and that blonde. Seems she was one of his students, a few years ago, at that college he works at. He'd never seen her with the war paint on. Nope, it wasn't Eliot."

"The Pennimans?"

"I thought of them a while. Guess he'd of done it if he'd really thought the old lady'd burn the house. Say, remember what you told Mrs. Penniman, about her men folks being out that night? You hit it first time, Doc."

"Did Alice tell you she'd told me?"

He nodded.

"Alice and Sam. Guess they won't make any trouble about his buying the place now, so's the young folks can live in it."

"I guess not," I said, knowing that that was just what they intended to do. "Did you think it was old John?"

"No, but he had chance enough. You know about him seeing Lafayette down there, with one of the old Wyndham dames? I just guessed that was the old lady hiding the loot. She done pretty well on that racket, now. The pearls was next. They'd of brought $2,500 or so. Good pickings. Nope, it wasn't old John I was thinking of in the back of my head."

"Gail?"

"Nope. She'd of done as well as the next, but it wasn't her."

"Richard?"

"He was my best bet until I found out the will wasn't signed."

"How'd you find that out?"

"Old girl's last lawyer."

"Oh."

"Nope, it wasn't none of them. I thought it was you did it, Doc, I sure did. And I ain't kidding you. You had the dope, you was there, you wouldn't give the certificate because the girl had seen the dog and you didn't want blackmail worked on you. Then I took half a look at the old judge and I could see he had a bum heart, and here you was acting as if you didn't know it. I thought all the while it was you leading me onto him because he was due to pass out any minute."

"Well," I said, "I'm sorry I misled you. I just never paid any attention to him. You must think I'm a rotten doctor."

"Nope," he said. "I guess you're maybe a right good woman doctor."

I smiled.

"Well," I said, "I've got to get home. Come and see me some time when you're down."

Lieutenant Kelly didn't move. He was thinking about something—and I couldn't go through the door with him in front of it.

"Just studyin'?" I said.

He looked up, and grinned suddenly.

"Y' know, Doc," he said, "I still ain't so sure about you. You really got the nerve to do it, you know, Doc. But hell, anyhow, it's all in the day's work. So long, Doc!"

"I really didn't do it," I said.

We shook hands heartily. It was then that he said, "Anyhow, Doc, you got a friend in me whenever you need one. All you got to do is just call Lieutenant Joseph Kelly at the Division of Detectives in Baltimore, and I'll be right with you."

Late that afternoon I was sitting in my office alone, having just finished the day's toll of casual patients.

Outside I could hear Estaphine talking over the garden fence to Mrs. West's cook, who was taking in the clothes from the line.

" 'Deed, Miss Liza, an' it's been mighty hard on the Doctuh," Estaphine was saying.

" 'Deed an' Ah should think it'd be. Him dyin' himself lak that jus' on a sudden."

" 'Tain't that so much as the way Miss Gail done acted."

Estaphine was really in her grandest manner.

"Yo' don' tell me! Ain' she want her marry Mistuh Nat? They tell me he got moah money'n he know what to do with."

" 'Deed 'n that's true an' we don' min' that. It ain' that, it's the *way* she done it. Runnin' off to a judge of the peace lak she was nobody! We's been countin' fo' yeahs on a formula weddin' fo' that chile. The doctuh's jus' all cut up 'bout it. 'Deed 'n she is, Miss Liza."

CPSIA information can be obtained
at www.ICGtesting.com
Printed in the USA
LVHW101424080222
710584LV00010B/109